BIBLIOPHILIA

An Epistolary Novel of
One Man's Obsession
with Book Collecting

BIBLIO

PHILIA

N. JOHN HALL

DAVID R. GODINE
Publisher · Boston

First published in 2016 by
DAVID R. GODINE · *Publisher*
Post Office Box 450
Jaffrey, New Hampshire 03452
www.godine.com

LIBRARY OF CONGRESS CATALOGING-IN-PUBLICATION DATA

Names: Hall, N. John, author.
Title: Bibliophilia : one man's obsession with book collecting / a novel by
N. John Hall.
Description: Jaffrey, New Hampshire : David R. Godine, [2016]
Identifiers: LCCN 2015050801| ISBN 9781567925616 (alk. paper) |
ISBN 1567925618 (alk. paper)
Subjects: LCSH: Book collectors—Fiction | Bibliomania—Fiction. |
GSAFD: Epistolary fiction.
Classification: LCC PS3608.A54745 B53 2016 | DDC 813/.6—dc23
LC record available at https://lccn.loc.gov/2015050801

FIRST EDITION
Printed in the United States of America

With thanks to
  Bob Call
  David Gordon
  Daniel Lowenthal
  Amy Millard
  Giles Harvey
  Mark Samuels Lasner
  Meryl Koopersmith

CHAPTER ONE

From: L.Dickerson@verizon.net
To: Nicholls@christies.co.uk
September 18, 2011

Dear Stephen

Are you still selling Cezannes for millions? I hope so. And Charlie is selling expensive books and manuscripts? I also hope there are no hard feelings. You tell me there are not and that Christie's made plenty on selling most of my letters. I have managed to keep that $400,000 I made in 2008 from that Phillip Osgood guy almost intact. I decided that buying manuscripts was not for me – too expensive. And then the market "went south" – as we say over here.

Now for my news. I'm going to be in touch with you (or rather mostly with Charlie), not about selling but about buying. I am going to become a rare book collector. What do you think of that? Not going to spend the whole $400,000 of course, just a reasonable amount. It will be a long long· while before I can even think of going after something expensive at auction.

Yours
Larry

27 East 13th Street Apt 12/B
New York NY 10003

*

3

From: Nicholls@christies.co.uk
To: L.Dickerson@verizon.net
21 September 2011

Dear Larry

Nice to hear from you. It's been three or four years, right? Things go well with me and with Christie's. The terrible financial turndown hasn't really affected the market for people with wealth. I mean of course my clients, not myself.

Tell me more, reasonably more (a joke), about your plans for becoming a book collector. You can't just collect books in general. You need a focus. But doubtless you already know this. Are you still crazy about your Victorian novelists? Are they the ones you intend to collect? If you are talking first editions and serialized parts, these can be very expensive. Have you told Charlie about your plans? That's her department, Books and Manuscripts.

And of course yes, one more time, no hard feelings. You made $400,000 on your great great grandfather's manuscript letters, and I myself told you, off the record, to do so. We explained to you that an auction house could not promise to meet Osgood's figure, and indeed that we thought the letters would fetch considerably less. On the other hand, Christie's got sizable commissions on the lots Osgood did not sell privately and which we eventually auctioned for him, all of which we managed to dispose of at good prices. I think Osgood did little more than break even, but I can't tell for sure and can't of course ask him.

I should not at all mind corresponding occasionally with you and hearing of your collecting progress. Charlie will also be happy to hear from you. We both often think of you with affection.

When you do write, use my private email. It's still the same:
    Nicholls@btinternet.com

4

Best
Stephen
Associate Director
Christie's
8 King Street
London SW1Y 6QT

*

From: L.Dickerson@verizon.net
To: Nicholls@btinternet.com
September 22, 2011

Dear Stephen

Yes, I'm going to be in touch with Charlie, but figured I'd start with you. I have decided in my old age to help the "plasticity" of my brain by getting involved in something new – like book collecting. By old age I mean my middle, or late, sixties. Of course today the so-called experts claim old age only begins at 75 or 80. That's a lot of crap. I always read the obituaries and not too many people in their eighties or nineties are listed. Is it because they are all living? Fat chance. Most people approaching 75 are already dead. So I figure whatever I got left is icing on the cake.

I've become really good friends with that Irving Gross fellow who used to teach at the New School. In fact he still does, but now he is in their regular Literature Department, not just in Continuing Education, where I met him in the evenings. You remember I was boning up on my Victorian novelists? Jaysus, when I think that I had more than a hundred manuscript letters from Dickens, Thackeray, Trollope, George Eliot, Hardy, et al (as you taught me to say), it almost makes me dizzy. But I have no complaint of course because I made such a pile of dough by selling those letters that these novelists wrote to my great great grandfather. Gross will help me, but I hope I can prevail on Charlie to help me too.

Don't mean to bore your head off. I'll get in touch with Charlie right now.

Yours
Larry

5

PS You remember how I like PSs in emails. The phrase "icing on the cake" is a metaphor here, right? I know damn well it's not "ironic." Ever since you got me thinking about the real meanings of words, I get annoyed at hearing "ironic" being used to mean "coincidence." And I'm tempted to surrender on "enormity" meaning "bigness." And just recently I was talking with a <u>lawyer</u>, no less, and she used "irregardless." I give up, but you should stick to your verbal guns.

*

From: Nicholls@btinternet.com
To: L.Dickerson@verizon.net
24 September 2011

Dear Larry

I'll try to keep up the good fight regarding the meanings of words.

Stephen

*   *   *

From: L.Dickerson@verizon.net
To: Charlie.Dover@christies.co.uk
September 25, 2011

Dear Charlie

How are you? I gather they haven't yet made you a director or something. You're probably better off right there in Books and Manuscripts, handling the rare things with your own hands instead of pushing papers for headquarters. When are they sending you to New York again? We can have supper, or dinner – which is it?
How is your private life, if I dare ask? Don't mean to pry.
I have decided to become a book collector. So I may eventually even

end up <u>buying</u> something at auction – not too expensive of course – at Christie's, naturally. But bidding at auction is a long way off.

Send me word that you wouldn't mind occasionally shooting the breeze with me (I love that phrase, though I doubt Stephen does).

So here's my situation. My experience with all those Victorian novelists really got up my interest in books, and I already have quite a regular little library – chiefly paperbacks of "my" Victorian novelists as connected with my great great grandfather's correspondence. And I have biographies of those novelists – Dickens, Thackeray, Hardy, Trollope (who wrote more novels than the others combined), George Eliot, et al. And you remember how I managed, with help from a freelance editor, to put transcriptions of them together in a little book, <u>The MacDowell Correspondence</u>, published by a small independent press here. But did I ever tell you – I can't remember if I did – that my edition of my gggf's letters got a "Briefly Noted" review in <u>The New Yorker</u>? Yeah, about 100 words, but still very nice. I figure that Briefly Noted was responsible for almost all the copies we sold. (Except if you count a nice, also short, but good review, in an online thing called "Bookslut." Such a name, but it's a sign of the times, I guess.)

I have even bought some cheap unpainted bookshelves – I'll probably paint them white, and the building super will help me secure them to one of the walls in my living room. Maybe someday I will call this room "the library," a la Masterpiece Theater. Of course rows of hard cover books look better than rows of paperbacks, but what can you do? The unpainted furniture place was going out of business like a lot of other places around here.

So now I am going to start serious book collecting, Victorian books, the real thing. I have been making some inquiries and talking to people and getting some advice. This English professor Irving Gross is going to help me. We have become very good friends. But of course I'd love to count on some help from <u>you</u>, although I don't want to make a pest of myself. Now, I know, as Stephen needlessly reminded me, that a person can't just start collecting "books in general." That would be crazy. You need a focus, a <u>fairly narrow</u> focus, Gross says. You can't go collecting the "Victorian novel" – you'd be near a million dollars. He also said that collecting Victorian novels in first editions can be tricky because of serialization, either in "parts" or in magazines. He says Dickens is largely responsible for this. Had it not been for Dickens, practically all Victorian novels — according to Gross — would be in three volumes, "three deckers," as they are called.

Gross also made the point that in his view you should collect writers you <u>like</u>. That makes good sense to me. So for me it's going to be Trollope. After all, he is my favorite Victorian novelist, although my single favorite novel of all time is <u>Vanity Fair</u>. Now Trollope wrote about 70 books if you count things like his travel books and biographies and essays. But just the novels — 47 of them. I'll have a Lawrence Dickerson Trollope Collection. Sound good?

Gross warned me to buy nothing at first; he advised that I should just use the internet to get the lay of the land. But it's too late, I already picked up a few old Trollope books.

> Yours
> Larry

*

From: Charlie.Dover@christies.co.uk
To: L.Dickerson@verizon.net
27 September 2011

Dear Larry

Really good to hear from you. Stephen forwarded your email to me, and then I got my own from you. Of course we miss you, and for the last time, forget deserting to Osgood. For one thing, we didn't really think of it that way; rather we understood it as "enlightened self-interest" on your part. Besides, that's old news now, and, for that matter, everyone came out of it just fine: you with a considerable balance at your banker's, and Christie's with its share of commissions. Although, to be sure, we don't know about Phillip Osgood, but I suspect he did better than break even. He certainly did not lose money. As for your corresponding with me on your book collecting, absolutely. But as with Stephen in the old days, use my private email:

Charlie.Dover@duquest.co.uk

To start collecting books you really need some help. It is part art and part science. You don't want to be using trial and error; that would be throwing money away. As the old saying goes, "Let the buyer beware" (Stephen would use only the Latin: Caveat emptor). Buying is easy but tricky, while selling, on the other hand, is hard and often disappointing. Of course, at Christie's, there's little difficulty for us because we are really middlemen, advertising for our clients via catalogues and online listings.

You did tell me about the brief notice in <u>The New Yorker</u>. It's really a coup to land one of those four slots, considering the huge number of books from which they are selected each week. It's too bad they didn't do a "Talk of the Town" piece, which would have entailed their coming to your place, interviewing you, learning how you inherited that box of letters, etc. Still, the Briefly Noted review is a genuine honour.

More soon. I have some definite ideas as to how you should go about this, but before I go any further, you say you have already bought some Trollope titles? Which ones? Publishers and dates?

I'm doing very well here at Christie's. As to my personal life, I am doing fine. I'm still single, if that's what you're asking.

Yours
Charlie

Charlotte M. Dover
Books and Manuscripts
Christie's
8 King Street
London SW₁Y 6QT

From: L.Dickerson@verizon.net
To: Charlie.Dover@duquest.co.uk
September 28, 2011

Dear Charlie

Thanks. Great to hear from you. Seems like old times. Glad to hear you and your work are prospering.

Here are some of the Trollope books I have bought from a place called the Victoria Book Shop:

Last Chronicle of Barset, Smith Elder, 1869
Framley Parsonage, Smith Elder, 1872
Doctor Thorne, Chapman & Hall, 1865
Barchester Towers, Peoples' Editions, Longman, 1858
The Warden, New Edition, Longman, 1868

Then I went back a second time for:

The Way We Live Now, Harpers, 1875

I also saw a three-volume novel that I figured was pretty good at $60.00, Susan Hopley, Or Circumstantial Evidence, London, Saunders and Otley, 3 Volumes, 1841, by Catherine Crowe. I know most Victorian novels were published in this "three decker" form. So I figured I should have one. What do you think?

                              Larry

                    *

From: Charlie.Dover@duquest.co.uk
To: L.Dickerson@verizon.net
30 September 2011

Dear Larry

The first five Trollope books you bought are not first editions and are
worth very little – next to nothing. What did you pay for them?

The Way We Live Now (Harpers) is a first edition, but it is the first
American edition (New York), worth just a fraction of the first English
(London) edition.

As for the three decker: no one knows anything about Catherine Crowe
and or her novel Susan Hopley. I'm sorry to say it's just about worthless.
As you know, just because a book is old doesn't mean it's worth anything.

Charlie

*

From: L.Dickerson@verizon.net
To: Charlie.Dover@duquest.co.uk
September 30, 2011

Dear Charlie

   For the first five books I paid about $100 a piece. They varied from
$95 to $120. For The Way We Live Now (my American "first edition") I
paid closer to $200, all in all some $700. So, adding the three-decker, it
comes to about $760, total.

Larry

*

From: Charlie.Dover@duquest.co.uk
To: L.Dickerson@verizon.net
2 October 2011

Dear Larry

I hate to be the bearer of bad news, but the books you bought are of very little value. The first thing you must do is slow down.

As you are going to concentrate on Trollope, you should find on the net an old copy of a 1928 book (reprinted 1964), <u>Trollope: A Bibliography</u>, by Michael Sadleir. This bibliography will tell you more than you need to know. When, for example, we look at your favorite Trollope novel, <u>The Last Chronicle of Barset</u>, we learn that the novel was originally published in 32 weekly sixpenny parts (a very rare form). But for the time being at least you should not go after novels in serialized parts because they are so expensive. For the first book edition, which is what you will want, Sadleir gives you the entire text of the title page, including publisher, Smith Elder, place of publication, London, and even the street address of the publisher, plus the date in Roman numerals. We learn that the book was published in two volumes; we get the exact size in inches, and we are given the number of pages in each volume, and a list of the titles of the illustrations. We read that the binding is "powder blue, sand-grained cloth with a blocked in gold design of a church porch" – and much more.

You may find that copies of any notable Victorian novel in original bindings are very expensive. Rebound copies, often in handsome "¾ leather," are perfectly acceptable in a collection such as you envision.

Trollope can be very expensive.

Charlie

*

From: L.Dickerson@verizon.net
To: Charlie.Dover@duquest.co.uk
October 2, 2011

Dear Charlie

    Christ, you mean I really took a shellacking on those books?
    OK. I'll follow through on your suggestion about Sadleir. And thanks for the long email.

Larry

*

From: Charlie.Dover@duquest.co.uk
To: L.Dickerson@verizon.net
5 October 2011

Dear Larry

Re the "shellacking," I'm afraid so. One way to check for sure is to have the books appraised. (But not at the place where you bought them.) Take them to the Argosy Book Store. It's on East 59th Street.

Charlie

*

From: L.Dickerson@verizon.net
To: Charlie.Dover@duquest.co.uk
October 7, 2011

Dear Charlie

    Well, I'm back from the Argosy Book Store. They told me the books were worth less than $10 each! (The New York first edition of The Way

13

We Live Now was just a tad better, $30. So only that one book counts as a real "collectible.") Boy, this is discouraging. As for the unknown three-decker, they didn't want it at any price. Fircrissakes, I don't think I could have given the goddam thing to them.

Larry

I'm going to follow your instructions closely. I'll be armed with the Sadleir Bibliography before I even think about buying another Trollope book.

*

From: Charlie.Dover@duquest.co.uk
To: L.Dickerson@verizon.net
9 October 2011

Dear Larry

Well, take your time. So you got off to a bad start. You want English first editions and not American editions. That's where the value is. But it's value over time – you can't immediately sell even a true first edition and get your money back. You are getting first editions not for resale – i.e., to make a profit – rather, you are buying them as a collector, to keep in a collection. Years down the road chances are they will have grown in value, but at this point you must not look at books as an investment. Although some people do collect books as an investment, it's not a good idea. And while most rare books rise in value, some of them in the long run go out of fashion. Supply and demand. Galsworthy, for instance, has gone far down in price.

Here's one reason why there are many more American firsts than English firsts. There are two ways to sell books (and many other commodities): either produce a few books and sell them at a high price; or, produce many copies and sell them at a cheap price. Thus, using an example I heard some years ago about an architecture book from London's Yale University

Press, the choice was to print 60 copies and sell them for £100 each; or, to print 1000 copies (paperback, but all else identical) and sell them for £6. The net gross in both cases was the same, £6,000. All publishers must estimate the market and follow one path or the other, albeit usually with much less dramatically different figures.

Nineteenth-century English publishers of novels followed the low print run, high price formula; the Americans (e.g. Harpers) followed the high print run, low price formula. Most American novels of the period were sold for $1.00 or $1.50. The British publishers, following the small print run practice, charged usually 31s (shillings) 6d (pennies). This monetary system is confusing to us: a pound contained 20 shillings, and a shilling contained twelve pennies. So, put another way, the novel's price was £1 11s 6d; this figure also amounted to a guinea and a half (a guinea being equivalent of a pound and a shilling). The decimal system is infinitely easier, but of course you are an expert on that. Trollope's character Plantagenet Palliser worked for years, unsuccessfully, trying to convert the ancient British coinage system to the decimal system. Decimal coinage came to us only in the early 1970s. Excuse that digression.

The point is that a three volume novel, like Oliver Twist, at 31s 6d came to (figuring the British pound at $5) eight times as much as an American copy of the book, where low price, large volume was the publishing practice. (There were also more people able to read in the U.S.)

However, one great advantage of the English system – high price, low print run – was that a publisher could afford to take on many more novels. He was not taking a great risk, for example, in printing 200 copies and selling only 190 copies (as was the case for Trollope's first novel, in 1847). Hence there were many more English than American novels published in the 19th century. An informed guess (by John Sutherland) says that during Victoria's long reign there were 60,000 novels published (and this figure does not include numerous Religious Tract Society novels). America published nothing close to this number of original novels. American publishers pirated popular British authors at no cost because there were no international copyright laws. Both Dickens and Trollope fought unsuccessfully for international copyright laws – these came only in the 1890s.

Slow down. And now that I think of it, besides having Sadleir's Bibliography, you should first, before buying anything, betake yourself to a rare book collection and see, firsthand, and handle (gingerly) the first editions. Most rare book libraries will have wonderful copies of everything you are thinking about. Here's my plan for you. I shall send an email to Isaac Gewirtz, curator of the Berg Collection, a small but jewel-like part of your great New York Public Library on Fifth Avenue and 42nd Street. I'll introduce you and tell him about your great great grandfather's letters, etc. Visiting the Berg is a little like getting into the holy of holies. Bring Isaac a copy of The MacDowell Correspondence, and then ask him to let you see a handful of Trollope first editions. He's very careful with his materials. Don't touch anything until he tells you that you may. This way you will get to see exactly what it is you are after, although on your budget you will probably be getting rebound copies of first editions because the books in their original bindings – not to mention serial parts – are exceedingly expensive these days.

Give it a few days, and I'll be in touch with Isaac. Then call him at the Berg: 212 930 8890.

Charlie

*

From: L.Dickerson@verizon.net
To: Charlie.Dover@duquest.co.uk
October 10, 2011

Dear Charlie

Thanks for all the dope on book publishing ratios, high price vs. low, pounds etc. That was your longest email ever, and don't think I don't appreciate it.

I have called and made an appointment with Isaac Gewirtz. Thanks for setting this up for me. He told me to come in next week but that I should first email him with a list of the half dozen or so Trollope books I'd like to see.

Larry

But now on another subject. I'm sorry that my language to Stephen as forwarded to you and in my email to you has been a little too salty, as we say. I get carried away typing. It's just that I feel you are such a good pal that I don't have to watch myself as much as I should.

From: Charlie.Dover@duquest.co.uk
To: L.Dickerson@verizon.net
20 October 2011

Larry

As for your language: Please, you must believe me when I say I don't mind your "salty" language. In fact I rather enjoy it. And to tell the truth, it is really not too salty. Never the F word or anything in that category. For the most part just "goddam," "hell," "Jaysus" and "fircrissakes." (Where did you find those last two spellings? The first sounds like James Joyce and the second like Ezra Pound.)

So just be yourself. Your language is a part of you.

Charlie

*

17

From: L.Dickerson@verizon.net
To: Charlie.Dover@duquest.co.uk
October 22, 2011

Dear Charlie

If you really mean it, hell, I won't watch my language but will just say what I feel about this and that. Do you really mean it?

Jaysus and fircrissakes: I thought I made up these words. Never read a word of Joyce or Pound. I understand they are tough sledding.

Larry

*

From: Charlie.Dover@duquest.co.uk
To: L.Dickerson@verizon.net
23 October 2011

Do I mean it? Of course I mean it. What the hell.

*

From: L.Dickerson@verizon.net
To: Charlie.Dover@duquest.co.uk
October 24, 2011

Dear Charlie

It's a deal. Your "What the hell" was very good.

Next week I'll get to the Berg and will report back.

In the meantime, something else entirely different: Now, guess what, Charlie m'dear? I've got a girlfriend! Although the word "girl" sounds strange for someone in her early sixties and a grandmother, like me – well I mean like me a grandparent (I've a son and two grandkids). And the best

part of all – get this – she's JEWISH. Not practicing much, thank god,
I could never go along with someone very religious, much less a religious
nut. But I always say that if you have to have a religion, Jewish is best
because, as I understand it, as a Jew you really don't have to believe very
much when you come right down to it.

The next best thing is that she is not looking to get married – divorced
she is, two times, and she's the one who did the divorcing. But, at least until
she divorces me – kidding – we're "a number," as they say over here. We
see each other on weekends, going on two years now. And we go to
movies. She loves movies, so I am seeing more than I used to. I am more for
staying at home, spending my TV time on sports. If everybody raves about a
movie, I get it later on Netflix. But my girlfriend, as I say, is crazy for going to
real movies, and she dragged me some time ago to see one called "Certified
Copy." After seeing it, I went back to see what The New Yorker had to say
about it (I keep ALL my copies). David Denby called it "a brilliant, endlessly
fascinating work" – this despite his assertion that the director is "playing
with us." Are the couple newly met or really married and separated fifteen
years ago? Myself, I like to know where I stand – or where the movie stands.
But the scenery makes you want to visit Italy. Maybe someday.

I thought you would get a kick out of this – not the movies, the
girlfriend business. She knows that I had a little secret crush on you (I
confessed) after I saw you for two days in New York, four years ago,
when you were here on Christie's business.

I remember that when you and I met, you told me you were Jewish,
and I stupidly said that I thought all English people were WASPs. That was
way off the mark – as if thinking that there can't be Jews of all different
nationalities. Remember the World War II joke – but then how could
you? – about the Japanese officer questioning a GI prisoner named Levy,
who won't give him any information: "Risten Revy, it's a rucky think for
you that I'm Jewish too."

Larry

*

19

From: Charlie.Dover@duquest.co.uk
To: L.Dickerson@verizon.net
27 October 2011

Dear Larry

Good for you. Does your girlfriend have a name?

I liked "Certified Copy." I don't get to as many movies as I'd like to. Always glad of a recommendation (from you and your New Yorker).

Charlie

I knew about your "little crush." Women know these things.

*

From: L.Dickerson@verizon.net
To: Charlie.Dover@duquest.co.uk
October 27, 2011

Dear Charlie

Right. Melanie. A nice name, right? Just goes to show that all Jews don't have to name their girls Miriam or Ruth or Esther.

My little crush – so you knew? Hope you didn't mind. How did you know?

Larry

Here's a movie you probably wouldn't like, despite The New Yorker, you being a woman and English. So I presume you don't care for American baseball, whereas I am a baseball nut. But this movie "Moneyball" isn't just about baseball, it's about business and statistics and computers; The New Yorker review says the movie could be used as a training manual at business schools.

*

From: Charlie.Dover@duquest.co.uk
To: L.Dickerson@verizon.net
27 October 2011

Dear Larry

On your little crush – of course I didn't mind. As I've already said, girls know these things. Shush on that subject.

I'll give "Moneyball" a miss. I await your report on the Berg.

In the meantime do a quick run through Abebooks, Amazon, eBay, Barnes and Noble, etc, not buying, just looking. And then visit some New York City rare book places online: the Argosy (of unhappy memory with reference to the value of your earlier purchases), and James Cummins; even the Strand Book Store has a rare book room; also Bauman (often considered rather "high end," but they occasionally have some good bargains). For that matter you could try Phillip Osgood. He would have only signed or inscribed books. But it would not hurt to see what he has. In London, there are many places, but I would recommend Maggs Bros and Jarndyce; both have searchable websites. Look for Trollope titles, and don't buy anything yet. Get a handle on prices. Then, after the Berg, go in person to a few rare book dealers in New York. Good Luck.

XO

Charlie

*

21

From: L.Dickerson@verizon.net
To: Charlie.Dover@duquest.co.uk
November 7, 2011

Dear Charlie,

    When I really get started, I'll go to James Cummins and the Strand. The Argosy too, but I hope they will forget that I was the guy who brought in those "early" (worthless) Trollope novels for appraisal. I'm a little leery of trying Osgood. He seems to deal in hundreds of thousands of dollars.

Larry

What the hell is XO?

*

From: Charlie.Dover@duquest.co.uk
To: L.Dickerson@verizon.net
8 November 2011

Larry

XO: only a little joke. It is computer language for a kiss and a hug – I trust your girlfriend won't mind.

Charlie

*

From: L.Dickerson@verizon.net
To: Charlie.Dover@duquest.co.uk
November 10, 2011

Dear Charlie

I'm back from the Berg. Holy of Holies indeed. The place is so locked up that Isaac Gewirtz has to use a key to let you in! Even though there was no one using the room when I visited him early at 10 AM, I felt I had to whisper.

I fished out of my bag a copy of The MacDowell Correspondence and gave it to him. This – your idea, though I like to think I would have thought of it too – was a bit of one-up-man-ship. He thanked me and then glanced through it and said it looked fascinating. In any case he was impressed. A good start. Gewirtz then inquired about the originals, and I told him I had sold them to Phillip Osgood. I asked if the Berg had any dealings with Osgood, and he said that yes, over the years he had occasionally dealt with him.

And there, all set out for me on long polished wooden tables, were copies of the books and serializations in parts that I said I'd like to see. (I was most careful and only picked up a book when he gave me the go-ahead.)

Gewirtz knows a hell of a lot, and I took it all in as best I could. Besides the Trollope books, he showed me Dickens's Pickwick Papers in monthly "parts" and explained how "revolutionary" this was – each part of twenty costing only a shilling, spread out over 20 months, instead of 31+ shillings all at once. Middle class people started to buy novels instead of renting them from libraries. (Working class people like farmers or factory workers making between 12 and 15 shillings a week would never buy a book – it would take the farmer three weeks' wages to buy one novel.) Pickwick was a bargain, piecemeal at a shilling a month spread out over nearly two years, and containing two illustrations per part (Victorians loved illustrations). Christ, you know all this, but I'm typing it out to keep it straight in my head and to impress you. Moreover the Dickens novel was much longer (and Victorians counted quantity), the equivalent of five volumes, each the size of one of the volumes in a traditional three-decker novel. Look at all I'm learning.

23

Gewirtz capped everything by showing me Thackeray's <u>Vanity Fair</u> in parts. It has over 200 drawings by Thackeray himself. But you of course know all this. I just want you to know that I know it. My head was spinning.

I thanked him profusely and was led out. You have to be let out again by key by the curator, otherwise you are locked in. Almost like a prison. But a wonderful prison. Thanks for clearing the way for me to get in. I feel I am entering another world – rare books. It's wonderful. But I am <u>itching</u> to BUY some of the things I have been reading about and seeing there at the Berg.

XO to you, too

Larry

CHAPTER TWO

From: L.Dickerson@verizon.net
To: Charlie.Dover@duquest.co.uk
November 21, 2011

Dear Charlie

   Gross is introducing me to an elderly retired professor who lives in
Scarsdale (very fancy pants, like Upper Montclair when I was a kid in New
Jersey) – this fellow who collects, or used to collect, the Victorians and
the early twentieth century. He is one Spencer Means. How is that for a
name? He also will show me books in a more relaxed environment than
the pressure-cooker Berg. I'm told that he has plenty of Trollope books.
   But before going up to see Means' collection, I'll wait until I have my
feet wet, with a few good purchases under my belt. Mixed metaphor?

                                          Larry

                            *

From: L.Dickerson@verizon.net
To: Charlie.Dover@duquest.co.uk
November 29, 2011

Dear Charlie

   OK. I am going through things on the internet looking for Trollope first
editions. Abebooks, which is supposed to be the largest online used book
seller, claims to list 1,700 first editions! But these include American first
editions, and "first edition thus," which I discover means first edition in
some new format that could have been "first published" last year.
   I went down this Abebooks list and got prices for about 30 of Trollope's

47 novels. I'm a little discouraged. There's a huge range in prices — Last Chronicle goes for from $1,500 up to $8,000; there are supposed to be "good" copies of Phineas Finn for $2,500; Eustace Diamonds for $5,500; Prime Minister for $5,700. Later ones like Dr. Wortle's School, are somewhat cheaper. Barchester Towers, rebound, costs $2,500.

I had been thinking $300 - $500 a piece on average for Trollope first editions. I was way off. And I haven't yet seen any prices for his earliest novels.

Larry

The movie "Hugo" in 3-D didn't convert me to 3-D, though of course it is pretty spectacular in places. The review in The New Yorker had only some minor reservations, saying, "The emotional pull of the story is irresistible.... 'Hugo' is superbly playful." I think a movie history buff would get more out of it than someone like me.

From: Charlie.Dover@duquest.co.uk
To: L.Dickerson@verizon.net
1 December 2011

Dear Larry

Try not to be discouraged. Take your time. And, yes, your average price was way off. Trollope is expensive. Remember about print runs: Trollope's very first novel had a print run of about 200 (and not all sold), whereas Dickens's Pickwick had about 40,000. Even at the height of Trollope's popularity, his Last Chronicle had a print run of only 3,000 copies (of which the lending libraries took about half, pretty much spoiling those copies). Hence, the relative scarcity of Trollope first editions on the market.

Charlie

Movies in 3-D tend to put me off.

From: L.Dickerson@verizon.net
To: Charlie.Dover@duquest.co.uk
December 3, 2011

Dear Charlie

   I've followed up on your leads. After spending hours looking at prices, I figure $3,000 a piece for Trollope novels, 47 total. This would come to $141,000! Even if I settled for copies at $2,000 each, it would amount to $94,000.

                                                        Larry

*

From: Charlie.Dover@duquest.co.uk
To: L.Dickerson@verizon.net
6 December 2011

Dear Larry

Even so, do your overall figures include what might be called a "surcharge" for the first three extremely rare books – The Macdermots, The Kellys, and La Vendée? You'll not get these for $3,000 each.

Charlie

*

27

From: L.Dickerson@verizon.net
To: Charlie.Dover@duquest.co.uk
December 9, 2011

Dear Charlie

    No. I have tried unsuccessfully to get prices on those three. You're saying that my figure of an "average" price as high as $3,000 for each Trollope book would be way off if I included the first three books?

                                                Larry

*

From: Charlie.Dover@duquest.co.uk
To: L.Dickerson@verizon.net
10 December 2011

Indeed it would.

*

From: L.Dickerson@verizon.net
To: Charlie.Dover@duquest.co.uk
December 15, 2011

Dear Charlie

    Although by now my search is just academic, I have gone through dozens of individual dealers, plus the Antique Booksellers Association of America (the ABAA, as you know) and the International League of Antiquarian Book Sellers. The first three Trollope novels seem rarer than Shakespeare 1st editions. From what I can see, real first editions for these three books are simply not out there.
    So what prices do I put on these non-existent books – $50,000 to

28

$100,000 each? Jaysus. So an "average" Trollope first edition price doesn't exist. My figures were way off, if you average in these unaverageable books.

The truth is you were right to hint that Trollope is out of reach unless I were thinking of investing the entire $400,000 in this book project, which of course I am not even considering. I was thinking more like $25,000, tops. Even that figure really shocks me.

It's all very discouraging.

Larry

*

From: Charlie.Dover@duquest.co.uk
To: L.Dickerson@verizon.net
17 December 2011

Dear Larry

My suggestion for you is this: collect just a dozen or so high points of the Victorian novel and do this in sync with your great great grandfather's letters as mentioning these titles. If I recall, Dickens is mentioned chiefly via David Copperfield; Hardy mainly through Tess; George Eliot through The Mill on the Floss, etc. Have your Victorian book collection complement your MacDowell letters. That will give your collection a unity and also a finishing point, at which time you can perhaps collect other, later, more reasonably priced authors. You will probably have to be satisfied with rebound books. Truly wealthy collectors want only original bindings, usually referred to as boards. These original bindings were often very flimsy, and those Victorians who could afford it had their books rebound, often in attractive leather bindings. Ironically, today these expensive leather-bound books are less desirable than those in the original flimsy boards. Moreover, it's hard to find the latter in good condition; hence, they are very expensive.

Charlie

*

From: L.Dickerson@verizon.net
To: Charlie.Dover@duquest.co.uk
December 18, 2011

Dear Charlie

   Christ, that sounds like a marvelous idea – connecting my collecting to novels highlighted in the MacDowell letters.
   Here's what I am going to do. First, I'll buy a first edition of my favorite Victorian novel, <u>Vanity Fair</u>, which was also the most prominently mentioned book in the MacDowell letters.
   And next, my favorite Trollope novel, <u>The Last Chronicle of Barset</u>.
   These I find can be had in fairly good condition, rebound, for about $1,500-$2,000 each. So I will have these two keystone books to start with.

                                          Larry

CHAPTER THREE

From: L.Dickerson@verizon.net
To: Charlie.Dover@duquest.co.uk
December 23, 2011

Dear Charlie

I've bought my first real first edition! A Christmas present to myself. (I'd wish you a Merry Christmas, but you're Jewish. I know, that's silly.)

Anyway, I bought my first real collector's book from James Cummins, with guidelines from you and from Irving Gross. It's a copy of Vanity Fair, condition "very good," rebound of course. I paid $1,500.

So here it is, my first first edition, a beautiful book, with 200 illustrations by Thackeray himself. I love the feel of it, the heft. I keep picking it up and gingerly opening it. Vanity Fair is lying right here on my desk. I'm in the collecting game. That leaves $398,500 to go. Just kidding. (I'm not counting the $760 wasted on those late editions that I impulsively bought before I knew anything about what I was doing.)

I'll be keeping a record of how much I pay for books. Do you mind if I occasionally keep you informed of my total outlay for this project? My other pals think I put too much emphasis on money. Of course I am no goddam millionaire just because I am buying a few books. But I have set a kind of target, which, as you know, is about $25,000, on first editions. I don't want to sound like a cheapskate (wonder what that "skate" means here?), but to me this is a lot of money. Cummins has a nice Last Chronicle rebound for $2,000. I'll get that book also. I didn't want to be buying more than one on my first visit.

Happy New Year.
Larry

Total outlay to date: $1,500.

*

From: Charlie.Dover@duquest.co.uk
To: L.Dickerson@verizon.net
2 January 2012

Dear Larry

Congratulations on getting started. It sounds like you are off to a good
start. James Cummins is a first-rate dealer. I have met him but never
visited his shop. And Vanity Fair of course is one of the most famous
books in the English language. I vaguely remember some survey taken a
few years ago (among whom I can't recall) that placed Vanity Fair first of
all English-language novels of any century. Naturally the make-up of those
polled determines the outcome of any survey.

Mention of condition reminds me to relay to you the old saying that in the
rare book business, there are three rules: Condition, Condition, Condition
(rather like Location, Location, Location in house-hunting). A beat-up copy
of a rare book is basically worthless, unless it's a Shakespeare First Folio or
something similar.

Keeping an accurate record of expenditures is absolutely the thing to do.
It's also a good idea to have some kind of working budget for a project
such as this – your figure of $25,000. Of course most projects of this kind
run over budget. And, yes, do from time to time let me know how your
outlay-to-date stands. It will be interesting to see if, or for how long, you
can keep within your proposed budget. Moreover, you should know that
collectors keep on collecting. They don't just say – as when buying a car
for example – "I'll spend 20,000 pounds, and that's it"; instead, collectors
may limit themselves to a vague yearly budget, but even then if something
really desirable turns up, they will almost always run past that figure. More
importantly, collectors don't stop after one year.

Happy New Year to you, too.

Charlie

*

From: L.Dickerson@verizon.net
To: Charlie.Dover@duquest.co.uk
January 4, 2012

Dear Charlie

Here is a preliminary list of what first editions I am after, my target books as linked to my MacDowell letters:
Thackeray, Vanity Fair, Purchased
Dickens, David Copperfield
George Eliot, The Mill on the Floss
Trollope, The Last Chronicle, Just purchased from Cummins for $2,000; and Orley Farm
Hardy, Tess of the D'Urbervilles
Butler, Erewhon
Collins, The Woman in White
Gaskell, The Life of Charlotte Bronte and Wives and Daughters
Darwin, On the Origin of Species
Secondary possibilities and additional titles: J.S. Mill, On Liberty and Autobiography; Dickens, Great Expectations; Trollope, The Warden and Barchester Towers.

I take your point about budgeting being different for a collector than someone with a one-time thing. Maybe I should say $20,000 for the first year.

Larry

As for Cummins's shop, it's on the top floor of a seven story building on Madison Avenue and 62nd Street (high rent district, to say the least). It's very impressive, with wooden book cases up to the high ceiling and glass cases exhibiting special books. There is even a long sofa to sit on while looking at their catalogues or at books you might think of buying. He had, for example, a first edition of Uncle Tom's Cabin for $10,000; Moby Dick

33

for $27,000; and <u>Walden</u> for $25,000. Not my area of course and way beyond my budget. Jim Cummins himself was very friendly. He also has rebound copies of <u>The Warden</u> and <u>Barchester Towers</u>. But I first want <u>Orley Farm</u> and the other books on my "A List," above.

   Total Outlay to date: $3,500.

*

From: L.Dickerson@verizon.net
To: Charlie.Dover@duquest.co.uk
January 10, 2012

Dear Charlie

   <u>Tess of the D'Urbervilles</u> is such a favorite novel that the prices start at $12,000 and descend to $4,000. That's what you get for wanting a book everybody else wants. I am going to look at a copy for $4,200 at New York Rare Books, Inc. That's pretty steep for me, but it's high on my list.

   I'm looking at George Eliot's <u>The Mill on the Floss</u> in original cloth, 3 volumes. I see the color of the book is in one place described as "orange-brown" and in another as "cinnamon." Take your choice. Prices range for these copies from $4,200 down to $2,200 from Bauman Booksellers, and from Boston's Peter Stern, "with some foxing," at $1,600. (I've learned "foxing" is brown age spots on the pages.) A rebound copy costs $1,300. I'm thinking it over. I will probably go uptown and look at the Bauman copy. Bauman always advertises on the back page of the <u>New York Times Book Review</u>, where they offer things like Steinbeck's <u>Grapes of Wrath</u> at $14,000 or Margaret Mitchell's <u>Gone with the Wind</u>, inscribed, for $24,000.

   As you know <u>David Copperfield</u> was Dickens's own favorite novel. Prices for <u>David Copperfield</u> include $17,000 for parts, and down to $4900 in original cloth. I have my eye on a Manhattan Rare Book Company copy rebound for $2,000 – binding by Riviere. Hell, if I can do with a rebound copy of <u>Vanity Fair</u>, the greatest novel of them all, I can surely put up with a rebound <u>Copperfield</u>. I don't know binders, but Riviere is often mentioned on the net as a big deal.

                                                              Larry

From: L.Dickerson@verizon.net
To: Charlie.Dover@duquest.co.uk
January 15, 2012

Dear Charlie

   I'm going to get the Bauman <u>David Copperfield</u> and The Manhattan
Rare Book Company <u>Mill on the Floss.</u> I also sprung for <u>Tess</u>, my most
expensive purchase ever at $4,200. And, oh my, what a lot of cash I have
spent in the last two days. $8,400! For three books!

                                              Larry

O my God – the total outlay to date is $11,900.

And I'm really just getting started.

*

From: L.Dickerson@verizon.net
To: Charlie.Dover@duquest.co.uk
January 20, 2012

Dear Charlie,

   Excuse the bombardment: Mrs. Gaskell figures in the MacDowell
letters, so I am reading <u>Wives and Daughters</u> and enjoying it very much. It
reminds me a little of a Trollope novel. And the character of Roger
Hamley, I learn, draws to some degree on Charles Darwin, who had a
family connection with the Gaskells. That of course interests me. So I will
collect <u>Wives and Daughters</u>. Also, I'm getting Mrs. Gaskell's <u>Life of
Charlotte Bronte</u> – which so intrigued my great great grandfather,
especially for the controversies it started. These two Gaskell books (I'm
just learning to call them "titles") don't have as many entries on the

35

internet as, say, Dickens, or George Eliot, for the obvious reason that she was not as popular as they were.

There is a copy of <u>Wives and Daughters</u> for $2,000 inscribed from Mary Augusta Austen-Leigh to her sister Cassandra. I checked it out. This woman, Mary Augusta Austen-Leigh, wrote a biography of her great aunt – Jane Austen. This <u>Wives and Daughters</u> is described as an "association copy." I think I know what that means. This would be my first inscribed or signed book.

<u>The Life of Charlotte Bronte</u> at Abebooks starts at $2,400. Rebound copies can be had for $1,200; there is a copy in original cloth binding for only $975, this last not in the best condition, but it is a copy that belonged to Andrew Pears of the famous Victorian Pears' Soap Company. This brings up the question of how much previous ownership adds to or detracts from the book's value. I'd appreciate your slant on the subject.

I also have a huge biography (from the Strand Bookstore) of Elizabeth Gaskell – but I'm not planning on reading it – just consulting it.

Larry

*

From: Charlie.Dover@duquest.co.uk
To: L.Dickerson@verizon.net
25 January 2012

Dear Larry,

Your question about whether or rather how much ownership by a famous person counts can be a tricky one to answer. First of all, there are some collectors who don't want <u>anything</u> added to the first edition; they are even against "flat-signed" copies, ones where the author (usually after first crossing through his or her name on the title page) signs underneath his or her printed name. These particular fanatics consider any signature or bookplate or inscription as a desecration of what they are after, viz., a pure and unadulterated first edition as it came off the press. On the other hand, most collectors regard this as wrong-headed, and are delighted with flat-signed books.

Owners' signatures usually detract from the value of a book unless the owner is a famous person. That a book belonged to Dickens would greatly enhance its value. Any book.

As for inscribed books, you can boil it down to four variables: status of inscriber; status of the recipient; the value of the inscribed book; and the substance of the inscription. As for the date of the inscription, the closer to publication the better.

Here's a hypothetical all-around winner: Trollope inscribing The Last Chronicle (perhaps his most famous novel) to George Eliot, with this inscription: "For Mrs Lewes, / With admiration from a day-to-day hard-working novelist / to a novelist of genius, / Yours, / Anthony Trollope / September 3, 1867." An inscription like that with its implications, including his addressing her as Mrs Lewes, a name which she cherished, and his calling her a genius, would add "stratospherically" to the price of the book.

In regard to the Pears' Soap copy: the book itself is important and the ownership by Andrew Pears is not insignificant. After all, Pears' Soap is still with us, right? In the 1880s the company was given a huge boost when it acquired "Bubbles," by John Everett Millais, both the painting itself and the copyright. Millais you will recognize as the illustrator of four of Trollope's novels, including Orley Farm. The painting shows a little boy (Millais's grandson) blowing soap bubbles. Millais had no control over the painting, and Pears added their name to it and used the image in advertisements for decades. It became Millais's most well-known painting (it's certainly not his best). Some people dislike the painting for what they see as sentimentality; others admire it for its evocation of the brevity, the precariousness, of life. All deplore its use as advertising.

You can see how the Austen-Leigh item has two fairly significant plusses — Austen-Leigh herself, great-niece of Jane Austen, and the intrinsic value of Gaskell's Wives and Daughters. The sister and the inscription add little.

Thus, an association copy is simply one that gains in value by its connection to some famous person through an inscription or by ownership (including bookplates). Sorry to be so long winded.

Charlie

I repeat, slow down.

*

From: L.Dickerson@verizon.net
To: Charlie.Dover@duquest.co.uk
January 28, 2012

Dear Charlie

Thanks for the run down on previous ownership, inscriptions, etc. I certainly hope to eventually get some good "association copies," and especially inscribed copies. In fact I'm going to buy the Pears' Soap Life of Charlotte Bronte (I still can't do most of these goddam accents) and Jane Austen's great-niece's copy of Wives and Daughters inscribed to her sister. I'll have two association copies for a start in that direction. Of course I'd prefer a Trollope or Thackeray inscription, but that is probably out of the question.

Larry

Total outlay to date: $14,875.

I am already having buyer's remorse, especially over that $4,200 for Tess. It's like I'm using Monopoly money. You're right, I must slow down.

Shoot me a picture of "Bubbles." I went around the corner to a drug store and bought a bar of Pears' "Transparent Soap." It costs $1.99, and the label says the company is "200 years old." The soap is "Made in India." No sign of "Bubbles."

From: Charlie.Dover@duquest.co.uk
To: L.Dickerson@verizon.net
5 February 2012

Dear Larry

I haven't seen the copies but the associations with the Austen family and (a little less so) Pears' Soap seem a reasonable beginning for association copies.

But a problem arises in that signatures and inscriptions (especially brief inscriptions) are somewhat easily forged. You can read about forgeries in all sorts of books, but one readily available source is <u>Warmly Inscribed</u> by Lawrence and Nancy Goldstone.

Charlie

I herewith send you an image of Millais's <u>Bubbles</u>, with the Pears' Soap "desecration" thereupon.

From: L.Dickerson@verizon.net
To: Charlie.Dover@duquest.co.uk
February 10, 2012

Dear Charlie

I got the Goldstones' book <u>Warmly Inscribed</u>. Jaysus, reading that about the New England Forger almost made me change my mind about collecting inscribed copies. Although I guess that if you are a forger you are more likely to forge Hemingway or Fitzgerald than Augusta Austen-Leigh or Andrew Pears.

You know what? Even though my great great grandfather, Jeremy MacDowell, didn't correspond with Charlotte Bronte — she died five years before he started writing to his novelists — of course her name came up a few times and especially in connection with Mrs. Gaskell's biography. So I decided to look into getting a copy of <u>Jane Eyre</u>. <u>Jane Eyre</u> is one of those books millions of people have read — or have at least seen one of the movies based on it. So I checked out prices on the internet. <u>Now</u> we are talking auction-house prices. You can get a copy of the 1847, Smith Elder, London, first edition (rebound no less) for a mere $89,000. If you skip up to 1850, the 2nd edition, you're down to $4,000! Thanks but no thanks.

Larry

And thanks on <u>Bubbles</u>. Did I tell you I got a pretty nice <u>Orley Farm</u> for $2,100? I got it some time ago at the Argosy Book Store. The novel has forty plates by John Everett Millais —

I send you a typical example. I know you know these plates, and I am sending this just to make sure I know how to properly send scans.

Total outlay to date: $16,975.

Now I <u>am</u> going to slow down.

*

40

From: Charlie.Dover@duquest.co.uk
To: L.Dickerson@verizon.net
13 February 2012

Dear Larry

Jane Eyre has been called the first first-book "instant best seller" in the history of the English novel. Dickens had half a dozen best sellers before the Brontë book – but his popularity was not "instant" – it took quite a few issues of the serial publication before Pickwick, and Dickens, took off.

I have heard it said that the experience of Charlotte Brontë has encouraged hundreds of thousands of would-be writers to dream of publication and success. I have even somewhere seen her, only half-jokingly, "blamed" for many of the unpublished manuscripts that clutter the desks and studies and closets of countless would-be novelists.

Charlie

In the case of Orley Farm, the Millais drawings add considerably to the book's value. Trollope himself said these illustrations were "the best I have seen in any novel in any language." While resisting that hyperbole, we can still admire their excellence. As you know, the drawing you sent depicts Lady Mason's second trial for forgery, wherein she was again acquitted (although she is guilty). I have read that there are over 100 lawyers in Trollope's fiction and that a dozen of his novels turn on a court trial. But Orley Farm is his most detailed investigation into the workings of the law. More than half of Millais's plates concern "the great Orley Farm case." (It's one of my favorite novels.)

*

From: L.Dickerson@verizon.net
To: Charlie.Dover@duquest.co.uk
February 25, 2012

Dear Charlie

   You are the only one of my book people to know Phillip Osgood, so I write to tell you that just for the hell of it I made an appointment and went up to his shop, which I learned carries not just autographs and manuscripts but inscribed books. I had never seen his place, you know. Back about four years ago, we had lunch and exchanged a dozen emails, and I sent him all the MacDowell letters by insured mail, and he sent me a check for $400,000. His store is on the second floor on East 83rd Street near Lexington Avenue. It's like one big safe, but with files and books all over the place. Jesus, the prices. He showed me some amazing signed letters and autographs. Lincoln, Jefferson, JFK, Einstein. He said he was very glad to see me. I didn't dare ask him how well he did with selling my gggf's letters. He seemed a little edgy. Or maybe I was the one on edge. It was a little awkward.
   In any case, he says, "What can I do for you?" I told him (it wasn't easy because I still feel like an outsider in the rare book world) that I was collecting just a handful of Victorian novels, "high points," by Dickens, Trollope, Thackeray, George Eliot, Hardy – but only if the book is prominently mentioned in my MacDowell letters. I added that I feared he dealt with books out of my budget-range. He said, "You might be surprised," and asked me which books I had already collected. So I told him Vanity Fair, Trollope's Orley Farm and Last Chronicle, and Dickens's David Copperfield, and a few others. He wanted to know did I have any inscribed copies. So I told him about the Austen-Leigh Wives and Daughters and Pears Soap Life of Charlotte Bronte. He asked me whether I was especially fascinated with signed or inscribed copies, and I told him I thought it would be fantastic to collect a few more signed copies, copies signed by someone more important than the Pears Soap guy or Augusta Austen-Leigh. He asked about prices I was paying, and he said he thought that what I was paying for unsigned copies was a little high. Would I like him to keep an eye out for some signed copies? What was I looking for?

I told him <u>Erewhon</u>, <u>Barchester Towers</u> and <u>The Warden</u>, maybe <u>Great Expectations</u>, and, for that matter, maybe signed copies of books I already collected, like <u>Vanity Fair</u>, <u>David Copperfield</u>, <u>The Last Chronicle</u>, and <u>Orley Farm</u>. I asked him where he would get these rare items. "I have my sources," he says. "Trade secret." I asked if he would be willing to have me trade up by selling him my copy of, say, <u>Orley Farm</u>, for a signed or inscribed copy, with me paying only the difference in price — if it were not too expensive a difference. He said he thought we could "work something out" along those lines.

He agreed that Darwin's <u>Origin</u> would be out of sight.

What do you think?

Larry

*

From: Charlie.Dover@duquest.co.uk
To: L.Dickerson@verizon.net
28 February 2012

Dear Larry

It doesn't do any harm to find out what Phillip Osgood wants for inscribed copies. Autographs are his specialty, as you know. I have met him a few times, and he certainly seems to know his business.

Charlie

*

From: L.Dickerson@verizon.net
To: Charlie.Dover@duquest.co.uk
March 1, 2012

That is not exactly a ringing endorsement, your words on Osgood.

*

From: Charlie.Dover@duquest.co.uk
To: L.Dickerson@verizon.net
2 March 2012

Dear Larry

I find Phillip Osgood is overly polite. And I don't exactly relish that. He seems – oh, I don't know – a little facile, a little slick. But the fact that I don't especially care for him personally is nothing against his integrity or way of doing business. And he gave you top dollar for all those letters. Hope this makes things clearer.

Charlie

PS: On rereading this email to you I realize that my words, "The fact that I don't care for Osgood personally is nothing against his integrity," are drawing on Oscar Wilde's defense of a writer named Wainwright who was also a forger and poisoner: "The fact of a man being a poisoner is nothing against his prose." This is all mutatis mutandis – look that up. A fine phrase, and very helpful in making comparisons and arguments.

PPS: In prison Wainwright (a great dandy) is said to have admitted poisoning his sister-in-law: "It was a dreadful thing to do, but she had very thick ankles." Now this is all meant to be funny (by both Wainwright and Wilde in quoting him). As a twenty-first century woman I am not supposed to find it funny – but I do.

44

*

From: L.Dickerson@verizon.net
To: Charlie.Dover@duquest.co.uk
March 5, 2012

Dear Charlie

I know what you mean, or I think I do. I'll play my cards close to the vest in dealing with Osgood. "Mutatis mutandis" – nice phrase, making the changes that have to be made. I'll try to remember it.

Larry

As for Wainwright and his being a poisoner not detracting from his prose – it makes you think. I read recently that Degas was a big anti-Semite. Can we still like his little dancing ballet girls?

*

From: L.Dickerson@verizon.net
To: Charlie.Dover@duquest.co.uk
March 11, 2012

Dear Charlie

I heard from Osgood, and he suggested I bring in some of my Victorian books so that he could take a look at them. I lugged four big books up to his place. He looked at them almost carelessly. Then he said, "I located a nice Erewhon for $800, signed." I told him I knew from the internet that uninscribed copies of Erewhon go for about $350, so that that meant $450 for the signature. "That's right," he said. Not wanting to appear too eager, I told him that I would think about it. (And before I left he offered me, "as an old customer," a 10% discount on any books bought from him.

45

So I took <u>Erewhon</u> at $720.) Then he brought out a rebound but briefly inscribed copy of <u>Orley Farm</u>: "For Charles/ Yours truly,/ Any Trollope." Osgood has no idea who "Charles" is. I asked how much he would allow for my copy as a trade-in. "Oh," he says, "I'll exchange copies giving you what you paid for yours." I told him I paid $2,100. Then he says that his copy is $4,000, but he'll give me 10% off, and that comes to $3,600 – minus the $2,100 for my copy. And so for $1,500 I got an inscribed Trollope novel.

I told him what I had paid for <u>Tess</u>, and he said I had overpaid on that one. He told me again that he would keep a lookout for signed copies of the titles I had unsigned or ones I was still looking for. He asked me if I would leave my other three books with him for a week or so, in order that he might judge their condition, etc, against possible trade ins. I agreed.

So I left his shop with one signed new book, <u>Erewhon</u>, and a signed Trollope, <u>Orley Farm</u>. All told I left him a check for $2,200. This gives me a total of four signed or inscribed books in my Victorian collection. I am spending my money too fast, but I can't resist what looks like a good deal.

Yours

Larry

Total outlay to date: $19,195.

Clearly $20,000 won't do for my first year. I'll up it to $25,000.

*

From: Charlie.Dover@duquest.co.uk
To: L.Dickerson@verizon.net
12 March 2012

Larry

I have two words for you: slow down.

Charlie

And, yes on Degas' ballet girls.

*

From: L.Dickerson@verizon.net
To: Charlie.Dover@duquest.co.uk
March 17, 2012

Dear Charlie

   Yes, I must slow down my buying. But now for a personal matter. You
are the only one I could ask about this, especially you being a woman "and
all," as the kids say. Here's my problem. Melanie and I see each other
every weekend and occasionally for some event on a week night – and
vacations of course. But Melanie is beginning to think I am more in love
with book collecting than I am with her. That's not true. Although, as I've
read recently, "Perception is reality" – for the perceiver. And although she
appreciates books and reading, she is a very active person. If she could, she
would see two movies every night, four museums on weekends, and travel
to Europe every other month. She thinks I am becoming too absorbed in
staying home and reading and working on my Collection (note I now give
it a capital "C"). Any advice for your old pal? I certainly don't want to lose
her to some goddam book – by Anthony Trollope or anybody else.

                                        Larry

*

From: Charlie.Dover@duquest.co.uk
To: L.Dickerson@verizon.net
20 March 2012

Dear Larry

Nice of you to confide in me. I'm no marriage counselor. But of course
you're not married, and for that matter neither am I. Still, here's what I
suggest. Why not meet each other half way, which would amount to your

47

going out more often and being more willing to travel. Of course if you two came to London you could quietly research places connected with your MacDowell letters and at the same time be on holiday with Melanie. And go ahead – go to more shows, movies, etc.

Yours
Charlie

*

From: L.Dickerson@verizon.net
To: Charlie.Dover@duquest.co.uk
March 22, 2012

Dear Charlie

Christ, of course you're right, as per usual, but I thought I was doing pretty well. But aside from eating out – which we always do – I suppose we don't do much else except the occasional movie. We recently saw (a re-run) Woody Allen's "Midnight in Paris," which David Denby in the New Yorker said was a success, a "gently rapt fable, caressed with wonderment" and a "love letter" to Paris. For me just the opening camera shots to Sidney Bechet's soprano sax (I love early New Orleans jazz) meant I was going to love the movie. The film makes you want to visit Paris. I know, after London. But first, I will psych myself up to get out more, see shows, concerts, even museums.

Many thanks
Larry

CHAPTER FOUR

From: L.Dickerson@verizon.net
To: L.Hill@lincoln.oxford.edu.uk
March 27, 2012

Dear Leonard Hill

You remember me, I hope. You helped me out with questions about Victorian writers and especially with Darwin and Butler. The strange thing is, I've become a book collector. You probably guessed that I made a pile of money selling my great great grandfather's letters.

In the beginning I thought about collecting all 47 of Trollope's novels, but I soon discovered that that would be not only expensive, but pretty nearly impossible, regardless of the money. So instead I'm choosing high points from the Victorians as mentioned in my great great grandfather's letters – a first edition of a book or two from each novelist.

But as you will recall there were two from Darwin in that big batch of old letters I sold. So I went on line to look for On the Origin of Species, London, John Murray, 1859. Here's a sampling of what I find: The true first edition, that is, first edition, first printing – it's a steal at $225,000! The Argosy Bookstore here has a less good copy for $150,000. Of course the Origin has been called "the most important scientific book of the 19th century." A copy of the 1869 goddam fifth edition is $20,725, fircrissakes. An autograph dealer here in New York named Osgood has an inscribed Origin, third edition, for $150,000. On the other hand, a second issue of sixth edition 1872, 1873, which drops the "On" from the title, sounds to me like a real possibility at $1,275.

I guess I hardly know what my question is. Maybe I just wanted to say hello and ask you what you think of these prices.

Yours
Larry

49

Here's a scan of the title page of the book neither of us can afford, the book some claim is "the most important book ever written" – scientific or not.

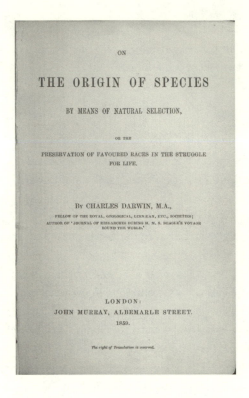

*

From: L.Hill@lincoln.oxford.edu.uk
To: L.Dickerson@verizon.net
2 April 2012

Dear Larry,

Of course I remember our correspondence. Most certainly I do. And the book you sent me of those marvelous letters to your great great grandfather. You'll be happy to hear that I refer to them in seminars.

So you've become a book collector. Good for you. I collect books though only in a minor way, but I know the thrill of getting a book one is after.

As for Darwin's Origin: it's good old supply and demand. The very first 1859 John Murray edition printed only 1,250 copies. Since then, it has been lauded to the skies; and "natural selection" has been called the greatest single idea in human history. These judgments are arguable, of course, but they are out there and have many adherents. However, even so, I am shocked at the price of $225,000. Part of the demand comes not just from collectors of Victorian books but from scientists, especially biologists. I cannot imagine, for example, that Richard Dawkins doesn't have or at least covet some early edition of the Origin.

Here's an interesting thing about all those different "editions" that publisher John Murray brought out in the original format, 1859-1873. These were truly new editions (not just reprintings, which some publishers then and now like to call "editions"). This is so because Darwin was a great reviser. Off the top of my head, I recall that among the six "original" editions there were more than two thousand sentences dropped or added; and over 15,000 changes in words or phrases. Some 75% of the text has been tinkered with over the years. So which is the "real" or "genuine," the authoritative Origin? You would think that was easy – the latest represents Darwin's final thinking. But all Darwin's revising has not convinced everyone that the question is settled. I am speaking of textual scholarship, not collecting, where clearly the first edition is most prized. Many scholars and lay people alike think that all Darwin's tinkering, much of it in answer to critics, actually detracted from the clarity of the original first edition.

Whether or not you should purchase the relatively inexpensive later edition I leave to your book collecting savvy.

Cordially
Leonard

Thanks for the scan from that famous book. We can only look at it.

51

From: L.Dickerson@verizon.net
To: L.Hill@lincoln.oxford.edu.uk
April 4, 2012

Dear Leonard

Thanks. I'm thinking it over. I'll probably go for the sixth edition – it has the same look as the earlier editions – same green cover, same publisher, John Murray, etc.

The only other Victorian writer from my great great grandfather's letters that I don't intend to get is Wilkie Collins – The Woman in White. I can't see paying $4,000 for a book I really don't like. To me, it's second-rate. Not that I don't enjoy reading a second-rate or even third-rate novel. But I certainly don't want to pay four grand for one. I recall that my great great grandfather didn't like The Woman in White, either.

Larry

CHAPTER FIVE

From: L.Dickerson@verizon.net
To: Charlie.Dover@duquest.co.uk
April 6, 2012

Dear Charlie

I visited the enemy camp today – Sotheby's. I hope you won't mind. Here's what happened: I was up seeing a knee specialist on East 72nd Street. But coming outside, I found Sotheby's right in front of me! Inside everyone welcomed me like I was some kind of millionaire client. And the beautiful young women minding the front counters were most helpful. The only exhibit on was Spanish Coins so I asked to see that even though I don't give a damn about old coins. It was on the 10th floor. There's also a nice little cafeteria on that floor. I looked around at the people eating and wondered if they were all millionaires. Or billionaires. I bravely sat down at a table and "bold as brass" (as my mother used to say) started looking through Sotheby's catalogues and a sort of fancy magazine hyping some past and some upcoming sales. This magazine lists everything from old masters at 4 to 6 million to that fraud Damien Hirst with an expected sale of $500,000 to $700,000 for a spot painting. Jaysus, such foolishness.

Oh, I learned from the magazine that the biggest seller for Sotheby's in 2011 was Clyfford Still – what the hell kind of a way to spell Clifford is that? Still's painting topped the year's best sellers at 61.6 million dollars, while a Correggio, an Old Master like that (I've been reading up a little on the history of art) – the Correggio got a measly 5.7 million dollars. If that isn't ass backwards – oops! – you tell me. And Still's "painting" is called "No. 1, 1949" and is of course "abstract." Oh Jesus, give me a break. Think of what good you could do with 61 million dollars. Clean water in bottles for half or India, or something.

I briefly did see some art. I asked a guard how to find the men's room, and she said go straight back there behind the scenes and keep turning right. All around me were paintings resting on stands, including a Lucian Freud. Is he any relation to the big Freud?

Oh yes, coming down in the elevator with me was a Sotheby's employee (he had a badge) with a dish of food and a bottle of fruit juice. I thought my god do they let him eat near the paintings? Since then a friend of mine, retired, who lives on my block, who used to be an art handler at Sotheby's, says if I had used the elevator a few more times I would have bumped into a wealthy celebrity or two. He says they are there all the time – Angelina Jolie, Brad Pitt, Madonna, Hugh Grant. Instead, I kept thinking how embarrassed I would have been to have bumped into Phillip Osgood – as if I had another $400,000 worth of letters to sell at auction. He has a way of making me nervous.

Back on the ground floor I saw that Sotheby's has a retail wine store, where you can get a bottle of Brouilly for $14.95. Christ, you'd think they wouldn't bother having a goddam regular wine store in a place that sells Cezannes and abstract paintings for $60 million each.

At the catalog counter I laid out $15 for that glossy Sotheby's at Auction magazine. "Would you like a bag?" "Oh, yes, sure." They gave me a Sotheby's bag for the magazine. The bag is more like a brief case, and in a color I don't know the name of – sort of purple but also gray – with the name SOTHEBY'S in silver lettering. It's so elegant that I was almost ashamed to be getting on the 72nd Street Crosstown Bus with the damned thing in my hand.

Larry

Melanie (who is an interior decorator) tells me the color of the bag is "iridescent aubergine."

*

From: Charlie.Dover@duquest.co.uk
To: L.Dickerson@verizon.net
9 April 2012

Dear Larry

1. Let's call Sotheby's a rival not an enemy. 2. Do try not being so intimidated by wealth. 3. Lucian Freud was Sigmund Freud's grandson.

Charlie

"Iridescent aubergine" sounds just right. It's nice that you have a girlfriend who could spot that.

*

From: L.Dickerson@verizon.net
To: Charlie.Dover@duquest.co.uk
April 10, 2012

Dear Charlie

Freud's grandson? Hell, that didn't hurt his reputation any, did it? Talk about "name recognition."

I find that Sotheby's is auctioning a copy of a special edition of The Importance of Being Earnest with an inscription from Oscar Wilde to his friend Robbie Ross. This goddam book is estimated to go from $80,000 to $120,000! Talk about the value of inscriptions. No wonder people are forging them.

Fussing around on the internet I see you people or rather Christie's New York sold a copy of Audubon's Birds of America for $7,922,500! (Stephen taught me it's bad form to use more than one exclamation mark.) For a book of bird drawings. I know that sounds like I'm a philistine, but I still say it's crazy.

Larry

55

*

From: Charlie.Dover@duquest.co.uk
To: L.Dickerson@verizon.net
15 April 2012

Dear Larry

Don't tell me about auction houses including ourselves underestimating prices. I was about to say that you were carrying coals to Newcastle. Every year there are things like a piece of the wedding cake of the abdicated King Edward VIII and his American wife Wallis Simpson. The evaluation was $500, and it went for $26,000.

Charlie

*

From: L.Dickerson@verizon.net
To: Charlie.Dover@duquest.co.uk
April 16, 2012

Dear Charlie

    Christ, the estimates missed it by a factor of 52. Must have been some rich fruitcake who bought it. (Pretty good, huh?)
    I had to look up "coals to Newcastle." Belaboring the obvious. But I take your point even if you wouldn't come right out and say so. You're right, what am I doing telling you about auction houses? Sorry. I'll try to confine myself to my collecting news.

Larry

I just read that Audubon, a great hunter, shot all the birds before he painted them. Not very politically correct.

56

*

From: Charlie.Dover@duquest.co.uk
To: L.Dickerson@verizon.net
23 April 2012

Dear Larry

No need to feel sorry. But do tell me of your latest purchases.

We keep an eye on other auctions. A letter or two back you mentioned Sotheby's selling an Oscar Wilde inscribed copy of The Importance of Being Earnest: Estimate, $80,000 to $120,000. The book, with buyer's premium, went for $364,500. Oscar Wilde is a hot author.

You and your girlfriend must come to London.

Charlie

*

From: L.Dickerson@verizon.net
To: Charlie.Dover@duquest.co.uk
April 24, 2012

Dear Charlie

    Thank god I am not interested in collecting Oscar Wilde. Madness.
    I bought a Darwin Origin 6th edition (original format) for $1,275.
    I must try to go easy. I almost dread another call from Osgood because he has such tempting books.

                                            Larry

Total outlay to date: $20,470.

Now that is 4/5 of my (extended) target for the first year. I really am going to call a halt, briefly.

CHAPTER SIX

From: L.Dickerson@verizon.net
To: smeans101@aol.com
April 25, 2012

Dear Spencer Means

   Irving Gross says he gave you my name and that you might be willing
to fill me in on some points about collecting first editions. I've started
aiming for about a dozen Victorian novels – high points of these authors. I
understand that you collect the Victorians and others on into the 20th
century. I don't really know any collectors. Gross of course is a college
teacher, and he knows a hell of a lot about English literature, but he is not
a collector.
   I would appreciate meeting you and seeing your collection.

                                    Yours sincerely
                                    Larry Dickerson

                        *

From: smeans101@aol.com
To: L.Dickerson@verizon.net
April 26, 2012

Dear Larry (and I'll be Spencer),

   Yes, my good friend Irving Gross says you are a beginning collector but
a serious one. Why don't you come up to my house next Wednesday?
Take the train to Scarsdale and have a cab bring you to 11 Sussex Place.

                                    Best wishes
                                    Spencer

*

From: smeans101@aol.com
To: L.Dickerson@verizon.net
May 3, 2012

Dear Larry

I enjoyed your visit and was very pleased to meet another collector. I think you are on the right track, viz., Victorian novels connected to your great great grandfather MacDowell's letters. And of course many thanks for the copy of that book. I'm well into reading it. Fascinating. What a marvelous thing that was, your inheriting those precious letters.

Yes, a soap company still owns Millais's "Bubbles," a portrait of his grandson (the boy grew up to be an admiral). Millais had intended the soap bubbles to illustrate the fleetingness of things, a trope early 17th century Dutch painters used. But the painting is still owned by Lever Bros, who took over Pears Soap in the early 20th century. The company has it on a long-term loan to the Lady Lever (still in the family, so to speak) Art Gallery in Liverpool. I keep an eye on Millais paintings and drawings. I'm most fortunate to have been able to obtain that watercolor version of one of his Trollope illustrations – from The Small House at Allington.

Best wishes
Spencer

As I told you, I know next to nothing about Phillip Osgood except that he is a well-known autograph dealer. The bulk of my collecting was done 20 to 30 years ago, long before he was on the scene.

*

From: L.Dickerson@verizon.net
To: smeans101@aol.com
May 3, 2012

Dear Spencer

Thanks for your letter. I was about to email a thank-you for having me up to Scarsdale to see you and your collection, and now you have first written to me. Well, thanks, for having me up and for all the information. It was wonderful to see all those books, most especially the Trollope first editions.

And then illustrations. To think that you have an original Millais drawing for Trollope. It must be terrific to have something like that on your walls – in addition to the books themselves. It's practically a museum piece. Come to think of it, of course it is a museum piece because his larger paintings are on the walls of many museums.

Larry

God knows when I'll ever have enough books collected to have you down to look at them. Of course you are welcome at any time you are in the city.

Someday I'm going to have some original art – connected to my book collecting.

* * *

From: smeans101@aol.com
To: Irving.Gross@ns.edu
May 4, 2012

Dear Irving

Your friend Dickerson, on your recommendation, was up here to see my books. And no, I'm not in the least writing to complain. He seemed a very likeable chap, fanatically interested in collecting. He was dying to ask me prices, I could sense that, but he behaved himself. Some of the things

61

he says and the questions he asks betray him as a Johnny-come-lately to books. But he knows this about himself, and he makes "no bones about it." He's learning plenty in what he calls his "old age." (From my viewpoint he doesn't know what old age is, yet.) He takes in everything, and with a kind of boyish enthusiasm – "This is really an original drawing? Christ, signed and everything!" He hides his shyness behind a bad-boy tongue. "I'll be damned – so this is a first edition of Pickwick Papers – in parts. Jesus. I saw a set in the Berg. But I hesitated to pick them up and examine them." This from the man who recently handled over a hundred big-name Victorian novelists' autograph letters.

He gave me a copy of The MacDowell Correspondence. He also said that he couldn't help telling me the book got a "Briefly Noted" notice in The New Yorker. He's very proud of that, as well he should be. The letters are altogether fascinating. He's very quick to mention the people who helped him, a man and a woman at Christie's London, and a freelance editor from Brooklyn, and you.

I like him.

He's been dealing with Phillip Osgood. I told him I know nothing of Osgood except that he is a well-known, high-end dealer, chiefly in letters and manuscripts, but apparently he handles inscribed books as well. Osgood, like so many people, was after my time.

Best wishes
Spencer

*

From: Irving.Gross@ns.edu
To: smeans101@aol.com
May 5, 2012

Dear Spencer

I'm glad you liked Larry Dickerson. I have become immensely fond of him. He is so anxious to learn and so assiduous in taking things in. I feel that we have a kind of crazy father/son relationship, he and I, with yours truly, though much younger than Larry, being the father and he the son.

I fear he may be going about collecting too quickly, not exactly recklessly, but too enthusiastically — especially with his latest interest in signed and inscribed copies. He has bought a number of signed books from Phillip Osgood — the dealer who gave him a generous $400,000 for his Victorian letters.

Irving

✳   ✳   ✳

From: L.Dickerson@verizon.net
To: Irving.Gross@ns.edu
May 6, 2012

Dear Irving

Thanks for introducing me to Spencer Means. I hadn't the nerve to ask him if people called him "Spence." But his collection bowled me over.

Larry

PS. I got another call to come up to see some things at Osgood's shop.

✳   ✳   ✳

From: L.Dickerson@verizon.net
To: Charlie.Dover@duquest.co.uk
May 9, 2012

Dear Charlie

   I'm really conflicted. You remember that my very first book was a rebound Vanity Fair, something I positively loved having. Well, Osgood has a Vanity Fair inscribed by Thackeray to some unknown person for $5,000. Again he would give me a "discount" of $500, plus allowing me $1,500 for what I paid for my copy. This means the signature would cost me $3,000. Outrageous, I know, but not if you check signed Vanity Fairs on the Abebooks network. And of course it is my all-time favorite Victorian novel – or novel of all time. What do you think?

Larry

*

From: Charlie.Dover@duquest.co.uk
To: L.Dickerson@verizon.net
10 May 2012

Dear Larry

That is not the kind of question I can answer. It's too personal and too much of a money question. Also, you know I have my personal reservations about Osgood. But, as before, this is nothing against his book selling.

Charlie

*

From: L.Dickerson@verizon.net
To: Charlie.Dover@duquest.co.uk
May 11, 2012

Dear Charlie

I bought the damn thing.

Larry

CHAPTER SEVEN

From: L.Dickerson@verizon.net
To: Irving.Gross@ns.edu
May 13, 2012

Dear Irving

   You remember that about two years ago The New Yorker did a little one paragraph "Briefly Noted" review of my MacDowell Correspondence? Of course you remember, because you called and told me about it. And how I immediately went out and bought half a dozen copies at the newsstand price? They were not exactly cheap at $6.00 per copy, but I figured what the hell, $36 wasn't a lot to pay for that kind of fame. Even if it was "brief" fame (I'll say it was brief). Too bad not many other places reviewed it. But The New Yorker was of course a big deal. And then, partly out of gratitude, you might say, I right then started subscribing to the magazine. I don't throw them out. So I must have about a hundred copies, starting with "my" issue. I love the covers and of course the cartoons, especially those by someone called "Gahan Wilson" – what kind of a name is Gahan anyway?
   I can't read the whole magazine of course, but occasionally I read a Profile, like the one debunking that crock Scientology. And I have been checking out the "Current Cinema" movie reviews.
   But I'm afraid I don't get some of the New Yorker cartoons – it's a generation gap. But the truth is I am a loyal subscriber of two years to a magazine that's been going, 50 issues a year, for 87 years. That means I missed approximately 4,250 copies. Not that I mean to try to catch up.

                                                        Larry

                              *

From:	Irving.Gross@ns.edu
To:	L.Dickerson@verizon.net
May 14, 2012

Dear Larry

You did indeed tell me about your subscribing to The New Yorker. And I'd bet that at the time I said that it was never too late to start taking that magazine. I've had English friends tell me that London has everything New York has except The New Yorker.

Irving

*

From:	L.Dickerson@verizon.net
To:	Irving.Gross@ns.edu
May 15, 2012

Dear Irving

I'm wondering if I should leave the Victorians for a while, since I have copies of most of the key books talked about in my great great grandfather's letters – you know, Vanity Fair, Tess of the d'Urbervilles, The Mill on the Floss, various Trollopes, etc. Plus David Copperfield, Erewhon, and Wives and Daughters (I even have a "late early edition" of The Origin of Species).

I was thinking about collecting some 20th century American writers. I figured they might be less expensive than the Victorians. (Of course I have not read a great many of them – I've only become a "book person" pretty recently, as you very well know.) But I was wrong. The most famous American novelists of the last century – Hemingway, Faulkner, and Fitzgerald – are just as expensive as the Victorians, in some cases more expensive because of the dust jacket business. Besides I haven't read these big guns except for Fitzgerald's The Great Gatsby, which everybody loves and reads and which comes in #2 on that list of Best 100 20th Century Novels. I have read some later 20th century novels, that is, a few by Philip Roth and the four <u>Rabbit</u> books by John Updike. I know Saul Bellow is right up there, too, but I couldn't get very far in his most famous book, <u>Herzog</u>. In any case, my preference goes to John Updike (except for Roth's <u>American Pastoral</u>, which I thought was terrific).

You remember when I was sick last winter and had bronchitis and you suggested that while I was laid up I read Updike's <u>Rabbit</u> books? They were like a drug – you keep coming back for more – one long book for each decade. I thought they were really great. Spencer Means has a lot of 20th century authors in his collection, including Updike. Updike was kind of like Trollope, Spencer tells me, in that he wrote an incredible number of good books. It seems collecting Updike all by himself would be a huge and expensive undertaking. And I don't know if I like him <u>that</u> much, that is, enough to devote myself entirely to collecting his works. In addition, it seems to me that this would be for me too narrow a focus. Collecting novels mentioned in my great great grandfather's letters provided a nice limited, but not too limited, focus. The 20th century seems so large, of course. I have no idea where to begin. Any thoughts?

Larry

*

From: Irving.Gross@ns.edu
To: L.Dickerson@verizon.net
May 16, 2012

Dear Larry

Here's an idea for you, sparked by your mention of Updike, a writer intimately connected with <u>The New Yorker</u>. Why don't you think of collecting high points from <u>New Yorker</u> writers – the early years. There are some great names, and they don't include Hemingway or Fitzgerald or Faulkner – all three off the charts expensive and who would bankrupt your budget in no time. This suggestion is somewhat selfish – if that is the word – on my part because the early New Yorker writers are a special scholarly interest of mine so I would know what I was doing in advising you on them. Moreover, I'd get a kick out of seeing these New Yorker first editions at your place. And you might take the same approach, more or less, as the one you used for the Victorians. That is, collect only "high points" among these New Yorker writers.

So here is where I would suggest you begin, especially as you are interested in drawings as well as books. You mentioned getting a look at some original drawings when you were visiting Spencer Means. He has a number of original James Thurber drawings – and also various other New Yorker cartoonists. Get a copy of James Thurber, the collected writings and drawings, a huge New American Library book. Just jump around in the book and look at the pictures. Don't attempt to read it end to end. Once you have poked around in it, get a modern paperback edition of Thurber's The Years with Ross (introduced and edited by a current New Yorker writer, Adam Gopnik). This book will throw light on the early history of The New Yorker, from its founding in 1925 by Harold Ross until his death in 1951. Ross is an endlessly fascinating figure: a seemingly hayseed philistine who was a genius editor.

Irving

＊

From: L.Dickerson@verizon.net
To: Irving.Gross@ns.edu
May 16, 2012

Dear Irving

   Christ, that's very much like my Victorian novelists strategy, as originally recommended by my friend Charlie at Christie's London. And I am very happy with the results. So I've ordered that American Library

<u>Thurber</u> and <u>The Years with Ross</u>. I have also, with some trepidation, told Osgood about my shift in focus.

Larry

*   *   *

From: L.Dickerson@verizon.net
To: Charlie.Dover@duquest.co.uk
May 17, 2012

Dear Charlie

    I have managed to collect maybe 90% of the MacDowell-related novels I wanted. Pretty good, eh? I have at least one for each author, except Wilkie Collins, who I don't like.
    But I am thinking of moving forward in a different direction altogether. I hope you don't think I am deserting English writers for American, but my pal Gross has got me interested in James Thurber and other <u>New Yorker</u> writers. He has me reading Thurber, and especially looking at his drawings – which I love.

Larry

Total outlay so far still $23,470.

*

From: Charlie.Dover@duquest.co.uk
To: L.Dickerson@verizon.net
19 May 2012

Dear Larry

No need to apologize for collecting American writers. Besides, we have actually handled some Thurber drawings. Do your research.

Charlie

*

From: L.Dickerson@verizon.net
To: Charlie.Dover@duquest.co.uk
May 20, 2012

Dear Charlie

Thanks. I'm going to do a little ground work on these New Yorker writers before plunging in as I foolishly did very early on with Trollope.

Larry

*

From: L.Dickerson@verizon.net
To: Charlie.Dover@duquest.co.uk
May 30, 2012

Dear Charlie

A follow up to our recent exchange about me getting out more with Melanie. We just passed the Memorial Day weekend here, and I really followed your advice and tried a lot of catching up in the getting-out department. We went to a Broadway play – a sort of musical (I hate all musicals except Guys and Dolls). This play, called The End of the Rainbow, was about Judy Garland's last days on earth, in 1968, in London. Then we rented Judy Garland's movie "A Star Is Born" (1954) and watched it as a follow-up to the play. Next we went to the Neue Galerie to see a Gustav

71

Klimt exhibit. Then we went to hear a New Orleans band playing in a dive somewhere in Williamsburg, Brooklyn. I forget what else we did, but I was certainly following your advice.

Part of my problem is that if I don't hear (from someone whose opinion I can trust) that a thing is any good, I don't want to go and find out. And I don't like violent or horror movies. This reminds me of an old joke from the 1960s where an Englishman says, "When I go to the movies, I go to be entertained. I don't go to the movies to see a lot of screaming, violence, horror, sex, and sodomy. I get all of that I want at home." I can be fussy. I couldn't watch Angela Lansbury to save my soul. Old-timer Cary Grant's voice grates on me. Also, Maya Angelou drives me crazy — her voice, so phony and affected-sounding. She's not an actress, of course, except in how she talks.

Larry

*

From: Charlie.Dover@duquest.co.co.uk
To: L.Dickerson@verizon.net
3 June 2012

Dear Larry

I agree with you on Angelou. In the TLS, the "Nota Bene" column (always signed simply "J.C." — Jesus Christ?) once referred to her as the "unspeakable Maya Angelou" — but if she didn't speak she wouldn't be unspeakable.

Charlie

*

From: L.Dickerson@verizon.net
To: Charlie.Dover@duquest.co.uk
June 5, 2012

Dear Charlie

   Another thing, Melanie and I are going to take a house for two weeks
in the Hamptons.

                              Larry

I just heard an excerpt from an interview with Maya Angelou on New
York Public Radio. She was asked which poetry she most enjoyed (or
most loved), and she said "Amiri Baraka, Nikki Giovanni, and some
Shakespeare."

                    *   *   *

From: L.Dickerson@verizon.net
To: Irving.Gross@ns.edu
July 16, 2012

Dear Irving

   I'm so obsessed with the possibilities of this new collecting focus that I
read all of that huge Thurber collection out there in the Hamptons and
went online to check prices of his many books. I especially love the
cartoons. I have ordered two inexpensive collections of his cartoons ($90
total – not "rare" at all). By the way, I can see how "The Secret Life of
Walter Mitty" is his most famous story. It's the only short story I ever read
that I wished was longer. I've just started The Years with Ross.

                              Larry

To tell the truth, I am glad to be back in the city – even though I enjoyed
the occasional visit to the beach in the Hamptons. But the money – where

73

else would you have to be ashamed of a V6 Honda Accord, rented and new – there among all the Mercedes, Lexuses, BMWs, even Bentleys (which I didn't think they even made anymore)?

*

From: Irving.Gross@ns.edu
To: L.Dickerson@verizon.net
July 17, 2012

Dear Larry

John Updike says, somewhere, that New Yorkers believe that people who live anywhere else in America are "only kidding."

Irving

*

From: L.Dickerson@verizon.net
To: Irving.Gross@ns.edu
July 25, 2012

Dear Irving

Yeah, New York's the place.
I wish I had been more interested in New Yorker writers and cartoonists when I was up there visiting Spencer Means. He has many writers from the first half of the 20th century, including New Yorker writers. In addition to his original Thurber drawings, he has various drawings from other New Yorker cartoonists. He even has some Gahan Wilson. I'd love to have some original drawings on my walls. I think Thurber's cartoons are terrific. Just a few lines do the trick.
Here's a scan of one of my favorites, "The Seal in the Bedroom."

Now you'll tell me it's everybody's favorite Thurber cartoon.

"All Right, Have It Your Way—You Heard a Seal Bark!"

Larry

As I start to think about collecting <u>New Yorker</u> writers, would you mind if from time to time I tell you the running total of money I have laid out? I've finished my Victorian novels – pretty much. Total outlay to date is $23,470. This means that collecting the Victorians damn near wiped out my target of $25,000. I'm now thinking of more like $30,000 for this first year. Priming the pump. I am presuming that 20th century books will not be as expensive as Dickens, Trollope, Hardy, et al. I may be wrong.

From: Irving.Gross@ns.edu
To: L.Dickerson@verizon.net
July 25, 2012

Dear Larry

"The Seal in the Bedroom" is almost everybody's favorite Thurber cartoon.

You asked me about some early New Yorker writers whom you might consider collecting, that is, looking into high points among them, in addition to Thurber and Updike (who isn't an "early" New Yorker writer). Here for starters are just some of the New Yorker writers I can recommend to you: E.B. White, Joseph Mitchell, and J.D. Salinger. First, read around in these writers. And also look into cartoonists Peter Arno, and Charles Addams. Thurber's drawings you already know about.

Irving

Sure, on the damages – but you have already spent much of your first-year so-called budget.

CHAPTER EIGHT

From: L.Dickerson@verizon.net
To: Irving.Gross@ns.edu
July 26, 2012

Dear Irving

Salinger! Thurber, yes, but Salinger! The Catcher in the Rye was one of
the few books I read in my younger days. Maybe 1966 or 1967 – that
must have been more than a dozen years after it came out and after about
ten million other people had read it. I can remember the teenage guy – I
forget his name, I will of course reread it immediately – who ended all his
sentences with "and all." Like the kids today ending (or beginning)
everything with "like." And he called everybody "old," including his
roommates and his teachers – who he dislikes – and even his younger
sister – who he loves. I forget her name: old Phyllis? No. I'll look it up.
Yeah, it's one of the few books I really liked back in those days. I'll look
into collecting Salinger. This is exciting.

Larry

*

From: Irving.Gross@ns.edu
To: L.Dickerson@verizon.net
July 27, 2012

Dear Larry

The teenager's name is Holden Caulfield; his ten-year-old sister is "old
Phoebe."

You will find, I'm pretty sure, that a true first edition of <u>Catcher in the Rye</u> will be <u>very</u> dear. He became so famous after that book that the print runs of his later books must have been (I'm only guessing) huge, and therefore these books will be considerably less expensive. Besides, he only published four books in all. Take your time. And visit places like the Argosy, Cummins, etc – even your old friend Osgood. Don't buy. You are new to this period.

Irving

*

From: L.Dickerson@verizon.net
To: Irving.Gross@ns.edu
July 28, 2012

Dear Irving

    Well, you sure were right about <u>Catcher in the Rye</u> prices. They are asking $55,000! – signed, but not even a "true first," that is, not a first printing. Then prices drop, and there is a lot of hair splitting about printings, issues, etc, and then re-bound copies. Collectors, as you know, don't want rebound 20th century books – where the dust jacket is crucial. And yet the Argosy Book Store has a rebound first edition for $2,500. You can get a "nice" copy of the second printing with a "facsimile dust jacket" for $500.
    The Argosy also has a Book-of-the-Month Club edition for only $230.00. I'm going to snap that up. And probably the facsimile jacket copy, too. Conversation pieces.
    I've started to reread <u>Catcher in the Rye</u> from an old 1961 paperback Signet edition. All the pages are brown and starting to crumble in your hands. (But a first edition of this cheap mass-market paperback costs $330.) This paperback is supposed to have sold only God knows how many millions of copies. I read that the cover picture of Holden Caulfield wearing his red hunting cap is "iconic" (as long as it is not "ironic"). I like

the book just as much as I did 40 years ago, and I am heading out now to the Three Lives Bookstore to get a newer, easier-to-read copy. I am about 100 pages into my beat-up old Signet edition.

But now I must ask you an embarrassing question. Just what the hell does the title "The Catcher in the Rye" mean? Thanks.

Larry

I called Osgood and told him I was switching to New Yorker writers, including Salinger. He's going to keep an eye out for books for me. Total outlay to date: $24,200.

*

From: Irving.Gross@ns.edu
To: L.Dickerson@verizon.net
July 29, 2012

Dear Larry

Do get a decent, readable copy of Catcher. There are splendid good-size type paperbacks of all four Salinger books, put out by Back Bay Books, which is really Little, Brown, of Boston (the original publishers). And you will see that these four books are very distinctive in that there are no puffs or claims or descriptions of any kind on the outside or inside of the books. All this simplicity was at Salinger's command. I know of no modern books published or reprinted like this, with not a single word of description or praise. Just title and author. The utter simplicity and lack of all puffing are part of the Salinger mystique.

As for the title: I could tell you to be patient; but instead, I'll say that when you get to page 224 in this Back Bay edition, Holden is talking with his ten-year-old sister, "old Phoebe." She is precocious (most children in Salinger's fiction are). Phoebe first corrects Holden's version from "If a body catch a body coming through the rye," to "If a body meet a body coming through the rye," and reminds him that the line is from a poem by Robert Burns. Holden resumes: "Anyway, I keep picturing all these little kids playing in some big field of rye and all. Thousands of kids, and nobody's around – nobody big, I mean, except me. And I'm standing on the edge of some crazy cliff. What I have to do, I have to catch everybody if they start to fall off the cliff – I mean they're running and they don't look where they are going and I have to come out from somewhere and <u>catch</u> them."

Irving

*

From: L.Dickerson@verizon.net
To: Irving.Gross@ns.edu
July 30, 2012

Dear Irving

Jaysus, I hate to admit it but rereading <u>The Catcher in the Rye</u> "wiped me out," especially the parts with his little sister, Old Phoebe. I got those nice Back Bay paperbacks of all four Salinger books. In <u>Nine Stories</u>, the very first story, "A Perfect Day for Bananafish," "really killed me," as Holden Caulfield would say.

I'm excited about getting these four books in first editions – I'll have a complete set of Salingers, the only author (so far) for whom I would have their complete works (I'd say "oeuvre" if I knew for sure how to spell that damn word without looking it up). The fact that Salinger published only these four books and just holed up somewhere in New Hampshire for 45 years and didn't publish anything else makes getting his complete works easy, especially for someone like me.

Larry

Total outlay to date: $24,200.

*

80

From: Irving.Gross@ns.edu
To: L.Dickerson@verizon.net
August 1, 2012

Dear Larry

You could supplement your Salinger books with a biography of Salinger.
There are a number of them, but Kenneth Slawenski's is probably the best.
It's in paperback and will tell you more than you need to know. That is, it
will give you not only all the known factual information about Salinger, but
it also tells you what Slawenski thinks you ought to think about what
everything means in the books: symbols, allegories, allusions, echoes, etc. I
myself don't recommend these interpretations to you. My advice is to
keep Slawenski handy but to concentrate on Salinger's four books – you
have already read two of them and enjoyed them for whatever they do
for you. In my view they all greatly reward rereading.

The last two books partly invoke Vedanta Hindu philosophy, but the
marvel is they are so good in spite of this.

Irving

*

From: L.Dickerson@verizon.net
To: Irving.Gross@ns.edu
August 2, 2012

Dear Irving

    I got a copy of Slawenski and leafing through it I find that he misuses
enormity: "the enormity of Salinger's talent," p. 249. Christ.

                                                    Larry

81

*

From: Irving.Gross@ns.edu
To: L.Dickerson@verizon.net
August 4, 2012

Dear Larry

Rather than having you read a book that misuses the word "enormity," let your old literature professor (a Salinger enthusiast) fill you in on a few biographical facts. Many people know that Salinger retreated from society, that he was interested in what you would call crack-pot notions – "spirituality," Hinduism, Buddhism, Zen, Eastern philosophy, but also urine drinking, beds facing north, Christian Science, Scientology, etc, and that he lived a famously reclusive life in rural Cornish, New Hampshire, until he died in 2010 at age 91. Few people know that he had a distinguished War record; he was with the first wave of troops on Utah Beach, fought on to Paris (where he had a drink with Hemingway at the Ritz). He then fought in the Battle of the Bulge, and was with the 12th Regiment when it liberated the concentration camps of Dachau. Salinger earned five battle stars and a presidential citation for bravery.

People your age all remember how in 1980 a mental case named David Chapman killed John Lennon. But they don't all remember that, after the shooting, Chapman sat down on the sidewalk and took out a copy of Catcher in the Rye and started reading it. Chapman later claimed the book had influenced his action; he also at times insisted he was Holden Caulfield.

A few months later, another psychotic, John Hinckley, shot President Reagan, and a copy of Catcher was discovered in his room. (There was a third incident in California, but I forget the details.) That out of sixty million readers, three misinterpreted the book as a call to violence is not Salinger's fault.

The bananafish story is from 1948. Yet this is really the <u>final</u> story of everything he published later about that most unusual Glass family, <u>Franny and Zooey</u> and <u>Raise High the Roof Beam, Carpenters</u> and <u>Seymour: An Introduction</u>. I say unusual because all seven of the children are precocious – and all of them appeared on a radio program called "It's a Wise Child." Seymour is the oldest, a kind of mystic, saint, Zen follower, and poet in Chinese and Japanese, adored by his brothers and sisters. And as you know, Seymour is the main character of the bananafish story. I don't know if way back in 1948 Salinger expected to make everything after <u>Catcher</u> a part of a never-completed Glass Family Saga. In any case, Salinger starts at the end, with Seymour's surprising death by suicide at age 31, while down in Florida on vacation with his wife.

Many readers and critics were disappointed in the Glass family books – they wanted another <u>Catcher in the Rye</u>. Although <u>Franny and Zooey</u> earned Salinger a <u>Time</u> cover, many critics were less than ecstatic. I give you an example copied out from "enormity" Slawenski: John Updike, on the front page of <u>The New York Times Book Review</u>, said, "Salinger loves the Glass children more than God loves them," but Updike closed his review saying that "the willingness such as Salinger's to risk excess on behalf of one's obsessions is what distinguishes artists from entertainers, and what makes some artists adventurers on behalf of us all." Nice, eh?

Pardon this enthusiasm. You can see from this lengthy email that I'm solidly in the Salinger camp.

Irving

*

From: L.Dickerson@verizon.net
To: Irving.Gross@ns.edu
August 5, 2012

Dear Irving

You know damned well there's no need to apologize for sending me of all people a long enthusiastic email. A thousand thanks.

I read on the net that every year hundreds of schools receive petitions to remove Catcher in the Rye from the classroom and the school library. The problem is largely the language. Get this: there are 245 "goddams" – one of my own favorites – in Catcher. The other objection is to the word "fuck," but the context shows how upset Holden is with seeing the words "Fuck you" on the wall in Phoebe's school. He would like to rub out all the "Fuck you" signs in the world, but he realizes it's no use "even if you had a million years."

Larry

PS I looked up that Random House list of 100 greatest novels of the 20th century – the one everybody hates unless their man is high on the list. Catcher in the Rye comes in at number 64. Not as high as I expected although ahead of A Farewell to Arms and Brideshead Revisited and another 34 novels. In case you forgot – professor – the top four are Ulysses, The Great Gatsby, A Portrait of the Artist as a Young Man, and Lolita. I have read numbers 2, 3, and 4. And I think I can see why they are so high. But Ulysses? I borrowed a library copy and could get nowhere at all. It made no sense to me. Christ, here I am trying to become a "bookman," and I can't read the novel everyone says is Number One in the entire 20th century.

*

From: Irving.Gross@ns.edu
To: L.Dickerson@verizon.net
August 7, 2012

Dear Larry

That Random House list was a good jumping off point for a lot of (usually silly) arguments. But before trying to answer your Ulysses question, let me ask you two questions: 1. Do you like Charlie Parker's jazz? 2. Do you consider yourself a leftist or a rightist (or in simpler terms, Democrat or Republican, liberal or conservative)?

Irving

*

From: L.Dickerson@verizon.net
To: Irving.Gross@ns.edu
August 8, 2012

Dear Irving

   Your questions relating to Ulysses. 1. I can say I pretty much hate the "advanced" music of Charlie Parker (give me George Lewis, or for that matter, Louis Armstrong or Sidney Bechet. New Orleans jazz is a hobby of mine). 2. Politically, as you well know, I am solidly on the left. Now please get back to me not understanding and therefore not liking Ulysses.

Larry

*

From: Irving.Gross@ns.edu
To: L.Dickerson@verizon.net
August 8, 2012

Dear Larry

Your answers demonstrate a pet idea of mine, namely that one can be politically liberal, progressive, leftist; while at the same time remaining aesthetically conservative, old fashioned, rightist. You yourself are plainly an example of this combination of liberal and conservative.

As for the reason you (and many others) don't like difficult High Modernist writing as in large parts of Joyce and Virginia Woolf, or progressive music whether in Charlie Parker or Philip Glass: the best explanation I know of was articulated by Philip Larkin, quoted just the other day in a review of his <u>Collected Poems</u>. The reviewer says that for Larkin, High Modernism in the various arts would in due course expose itself as "mystification and outrage." Larkin deplored the music of Charlie Parker and the art of Pound or Picasso, "not because they are new, but because they are irresponsible exploitations of technique in contradiction of human life as we know it." Such art "helps us neither to enjoy nor to endure. It will divert us as long as we are prepared to be mystified or outraged."

I'm not saying I agree with Larkin, but I certainly take his point. I expect that you, Larry, both take his point and subscribe to it.

Irving

*

From: L.Dickerson@verizon.net
To: Irving.Gross@ns.edu
August 9, 2012

Irving

You're damned right I subscribe to it.

Larry

CHAPTER NINE

From: L.Dickerson@verizon.net
To: Irving.Gross@ns.edu
August 11, 2012

Dear Irving

    I have by now carefully read all four Salinger books. As for my own personal enjoyment – after Catcher, of course – I prefer Franny and Raise High the Roof Beam to Zooey and Seymour: An Introduction. I guess I like the ones with more "story" in them. Among the short stories of course I think "A Perfect Day for Bananafish" is the best. Now you will tell me everybody thinks "Bananafish" his best short story.

Larry

Yesterday, watching the Olympics, I heard the NBC announcer say it was "ironic" that a runner had fallen on the anniversary of Mary Decker's fall during the 1984 Olympics. Should I give up on people who should know better using "ironic" to mean "coincidental?" Just to make sure I was not wrong, I looked up the word in the American Heritage Dictionary: there were seven distinct meanings for the word and thank God not one of them had anything to do with coincidence. No word from old Osgood. He must make enough money to take all of July and August off – probably in the Hamptons.

*

From: Irving.Gross@ns.edu
To: L.Dickerson@verizon.net
August 13, 2012

Dear Larry

Don't give up on announcers' misuse of words. Keep up the fight.

But, yes, I can tell you that most readers are said to think "Bananafish" the best of Salinger's short stories.

But listen to this: Slawenski says that Vladimir Nabokov (who also wrote much for The New Yorker) claimed that the bananafish story inspired Lolita. This is a complete exaggeration; Salinger's story may have added some impetus to Nabokov's writing of Lolita, but Nabokov had been thinking about and even publishing some similar-themed stories over many years.

Irving

Osgood's being away has probably enabled you to slow down a bit, which is probably a good thing.

*

From: L.Dickerson@verizon.net
To: Irving.Gross@ns.edu
August 14, 2012

Dear Irving

    A funny thing about Lolita being inspired by "A Perfect Day for Bananafish." My first reaction was that that was a lot of crap. On the other hand, I was so impressed by the story that I read parts of it aloud to Melanie. I read her just the second half of the story – skipping the phone conversation between Seymour's wife and her mother and the last paragraph where Seymour shoots himself in the head. I read just the episode with the little girl, who is staying in the same beach hotel as Seymour and his wife. The girl finds "See more glass" (as she so cutely calls him) on the beach, and he takes her out into the water to look for bananafish. It's lovely. When I finished reading, Melanie told me that while listening she had been afraid Seymour was going to molest the five-year-old girl, even though nothing could be further from Seymour's intention. So I suppose Nabokov could have said that <u>Lolita</u> drew partly on "Bananafish" for inspiration even though he came up with something so entirely different.

Of course, once you went and mentioned <u>Lolita</u> I went right out and got a video – the 1962 version, with James Mason. Terrible movie for anyone who has read the book. Way too much emphasis on Lolita's mother, ridiculously over-acted by Shelley Winters, and Lolita herself looks 18 from the start. The truth is that in 1962 you couldn't make a movie at all faithful to the book.

Two days later I got the 1997 version with Jeremy Irons, which was much better – the girl Lolita looks like a girl, and Irons is terrific as Humbert Humbert (nice name).

Larry

Just for the hell of it I looked up a first edition of <u>Lolita</u>, Olympia Press, Paris, 1955, two volumes, paper wrappers. The price is $10,000. Not as high as I expected, but way out of my range. On the other hand, there seem to be a lot of copies for sale. The Argosy has a less good copy for $2,200. But I'm not sure Nabokov comes within my collecting range.

From: Irving.Gross@ns.edu
To: L.Dickerson@verizon.net
August 17, 2012

Larry

Why not include Nabokov? He published innumerable stories, poems, autobiographical memories, and criticism in <u>The New Yorker</u>. Not Lolita of course, because it would never have passed by the puritanical reticence of Shawn. (In Roof Beam Salinger had Buddy Glass go into the bathroom to sit on the toilet seat to read Seymour's diary in private; the published version has him sitting on the edge of the tub.) Lolita was turned down by four big New York publishers before Nabokov took the manuscript to Paris.

Nabokov is an amazing figure, completely literate (and literary) in his native Russian, in French, and in English (which he learned to read as a child – even before he could read Russian). He was also a distinguished authority on butterflies and on chess. Americans today know him only for Lolita, but he published – I don't know – fifteen or twenty other novels, including Pale Fire, a kind of spoofy literary joke. As I recall, it also landed on the Random House list of 100 best novels of the 20th century. You could look it up.

His autobiography of his years before coming to America, in original form called Conclusive Evidence (i.e., evidence of his existence), came in final form to be called Speak, Memory. He had wanted it called Speak, Mnemosyne, but the publisher insisted people would never buy a book with a title they couldn't pronounce. It's considered one of the greatest autobiographies in any language.

When a short story of his was accepted by New Yorker fiction editor Katherine White, he was delighted but didn't foresee the New Yorker policy of extensive editing; he wrote to Edmund Wilson (who had brought him to the magazine) that "a man named Ross started to 'edit' my story." Nabokov then told Mrs. White that he could not admit of such "ridiculous and exasperating alterations." A middle ground was reached, but for the most part Nabokov successfully resisted New Yorker tinkering. I can recall one of Ross's queries to one of the installments of what became Speak, Memory, where Nabokov wrote of his childhood in St Petersburg, recalling "voices speaking, a walnut cracked, the click of the nut-cracker;" Ross wrote, "Were the Nabokovs a one-nutcracker family?" This suggestion Nabokov not only accepted but gleefully mentioned in his introduction to the 1966 edition. You can see Nabokov is another enthusiasm of mine.

Irving

91

*

From: L.Dickerson@verizon.net
To: Irving.Gross@ns.edu
August 20, 2012

Dear Irving

    Well, you certainly convinced me about Nabokov. I took the <u>Lolita</u> for $2,200, from Argosy.

    And, yes, <u>Pale Fire</u> is number 53 on that crazy old hit parade. That gives Nabokov two of the top 100. Two of the top 60, actually.

    I see that a signed first edition of <u>Speak, Memory</u>, 1951, goes for $10,000. An ordinary copy costs from $150 to $500. Signatures are really expensive.

    I've picked up an old, battered copy of <u>Speak, Memory</u> (former owner: Southern Methodist University Library) for about five dollars plus postage. What a book! What language! And what a memory.

Larry

Total outlay to date: $26,400.

*

From: Irving.Gross@ns.edu
To: L.Dickerson@verizon.net
August 21, 2012

Dear Larry

On <u>Speak, Memory</u> my advice is simply to immerse yourself in his ripe, flowery prose. Don't stop to look up words or you'll not get very far.

92

Curiously, Ross, such a stickler for clear and straightforward prose, became a champion of Nabokov's dense and sinuous writing. In the case of "Portrait of My Uncle," the first installment of what became <u>Speak, Memory</u>, Ross overruled his editors (including Mrs. White) and accepted this idiosyncratic, difficult, and unusual piece. Ross later said that there were twenty words he couldn't recognize in the first two pages. Of "Parks and Gardens" (the last chapter in the book), he said it was "the most remarkable emotional tour de force I ever read." He also said he was "astonished at the vehemence of the Freud reference," although it was "probably a wholesome thing." You'll find this on page 300 of the Putnam edition. Nabokov is writing of the passion male children have for things on wheels, especially railway trains: "Of course we know what the Viennese Quack thought of the matter. We will leave him and his fellow travelers to jog on, in their third-class carriage of thought, through the police state of sexual myth."

Irving

*

From: L.Dickerson@verizon.net
To: Irving.Gross@ns.edu
August 24, 2012

Dear Irving

    I have never read anything like <u>Speak, Memory</u>. (I know I say this about a lot of books.) I'm not saying it is the greatest thing I've read, at all, I'm just saying how really different it is from other kinds of writing that I've read. I will admit that like good old Harold Ross I constantly run into words I've not only never heard of but which I sometimes have trouble finding in a dictionary. Sometimes you can guess the meaning:

    "an almost discarnate feeling" = out of body?
    "consociative virtues" = associated with?

But how about?
   "ridiculous cacologist that I am"
   "our bebile old Benz"
   "my almost couvade-like concern"
   "Mystagogue"

Even more striking is his way of saying things vividly without difficult words:
   On never wanting to go to sleep: "I simply cannot get used to the nightly betrayal of reason, humanity, genius" (talk about self-esteem).
   On losing his virginity: "In one particular pine grove everything fell into place, I parted the fabric of fancy, I tasted reality."
   A particular man has "an unchaste vocabulary."
   A mirror is "badly disfigured but still alert."

                                        Mystagogically yours
                                        Larry

                    *   *   *

From: L.Dickerson@verizon.net
To: Charlie.Dover@duquest.co.uk
August 27, 2012

Dear Charlie

   Just a note to say hello and to tell you that I'm reading and collecting Nabokov – and that he begins Chapter Three of Speak, Memory as follows: "The kind of Russian family to which I belonged (50 servants, paintings of old masters on the walls, etc) – a kind now extinct – had among other virtues, a traditional leaning toward the comfortable products of Anglo-Saxon civilization." The prime example he offers is Pears' Soap! You will recall that I bought a copy of The Life of Charlotte Bronte owned by Andrew Pears.

                                        Larry

*

From: Charlie.Dover@duquest.co.uk
To: L.Dickerson@verizon.net
28 August 2012

Dear Larry

Well, Pears' Soap: a real compliment to British civilisation. Good to know that.

Charlie

CHAPTER TEN

From: L.Dickerson@verizon.net
To: Charlie.Dover@duquest.co.uk
August 29, 2012

Dear Charlie

    I have a question for you on dust jackets: What the hell is this all about? I know they are a 20th century thing, for the most part – no dust jackets for writers like Dickens, Thackeray, George Eliot, et al. But the value of dust jackets today for 20th century fiction is out of sight. Just for the fun of it, I looked up some famous 20th century books on the internet. I see, for example, Hemingway – a jacketless "true" first edition of The Sun Also Rises goes for $2,000, but with the dust jacket the price is $45,000! About 22 times as much. (Never mind a copy with an inscription – $200,000.) Then I looked for F. Scott Fitzgerald: a decent unjacketed copy of the first edition of The Great Gatsby goes for $5000; with dust jacket anywhere from $200,000 to $500,000! Isn't that crazy?

                                                     Larry

*

From: Charlie.Dover@duquest.co.co.uk
To: L.Dickerson@verizon.net
1 September 2012

Dear Larry

A first edition of a twentieth-century book, say Gatsby, without a dust jacket is in a very real sense not the entire book. Publishers will tell you that great care (and time) goes into the design of the cover: selecting an image (or opting for none), choosing the lettering style, determining the relative font size of title and author's name, etc. The text on the inner flaps, back and front, are carefully attended to, how to describe the work and how much to hype the author. The fussy and moneyed collector would no sooner buy a jacketless Gatsby than he would buy a copy from which the title page had been ripped out; in fact he would prefer the latter because a missing title page can be rather easily restored (although it would still be a serious mark against that copy). But the lack of a dust jacket he views as a radical fault. Of course from a purely literary standpoint, or from the reader's viewpoint, the text (including title) is all he needs. Not so for the serious collector, for whom the jacket is a sine qua non. As to the huge premium commanded by jacketed copies, this is simply the way the market has emerged. Early in the twentieth century dust jackets were not as much in demand as today. Remember too, that readers, especially years ago, discarded dust jackets. That said, the enormous difference in price between jacketed and unjacketed copies remains somewhat mysterious.

Wealthy people who have the book-collecting bug, that "gentle madness," can spend their money in ways that the ordinary person finds silly, even obscene. We at Christie's don't go around saying anything like that because middle-class citizens like Stephen and I, in working for Christie's, are part of the scene. We make our living (and, by the way, not at all rich livings) by catering to this madness. Moreover, when you do it all day long, you become indifferent to exorbitant prices.

Charlie

*

97

From: L.Dickerson@verizon.net
To: Charlie.Dover@duquest.co.uk
September 2, 2012

Dear Charlie

What happens when a collector or seller takes a "fine dust jacket" from a book that has, say, underlinings, bent pages, and other imperfections that greatly detract from the value of the book, and puts the good dust jacket on a different "fine, clean, bright almost like new" copy of the book? Is this easy to spot? Is the practice considered dishonest?

Larry

I had of course to look up <u>sine qua non</u>.

*

From: Charlie.Dover@duquest.co.uk
To: L.Dickerson@verizon.net
4 September 2012

Dear Larry

The practice is called "marrying." You marry a good dust jacket with a good copy heretofore jacketless. People disagree about the honesty of the practice. Fastidious deep-pocketed collectors are more likely to object to it. At Christie's the question doesn't really come up. We don't keep stock like a store. We auction what people give us to sell, "as is."

I can't recall that I myself was ever called on to arrange such a marriage. But a "proper marriage" can be a tricky thing. Dust jackets themselves also come in states with points, and for a correct marrying, you need the same printing for the book and for the jacket. If an author, for example, insists on having his picture removed from the back cover after the first printing (as Salinger did with Catcher), and you find a true first edition with a photoless dust jacket, you should see a problem. Certainly a knowledgeable collector would spot it.

Consider too, that there are avid readers, who, though not at all collectors, do not like to tarnish or disfigure the dust jacket of a new book. Rather, they put the jacket aside until they are finished reading the book. The jacket will sometimes be in better condition than the book, and this jacket ends up a candidate for marriage to a copy of the book in better condition.

Charlie

*

From: L.Dickerson@verizon.net
To: Charlie.Dover@duquest.co.uk
September 5, 2012

Dear Charlie

   That clears it up nicely, except the unanswerable question of the incredible difference between a $5,000 jacketless copy of Gatsby vs a $500,000 copy, with jacket. And, as it's unanswerable – the hell with it.

                                        Larry

PS What about "ex-libris" copies? One of my Victorian books has an "Ex Libris" book plate from someone evidently unknown today.

*

From: Charlie.Dover@duquest.co.co.uk
To: L.Dickerson@verizon.net
8 September 2012

Dear Larry

If the book has an "Ex-Library" sticker of a previous owner, this usually detracts from the book's value unless the sticker belonged to a famous person. An exception would be a beautifully engraved bookplate, even if commissioned by someone unknown today. Remember too that public librarians used to discard dust jackets, paint call numbers on the spine, and blind stamp or rubber stamp the name of library, pretty much ruining the book and making good copies rarer. Libraries are more careful now, but they still disfigure books. This is partly why "ex-library" copies of a book are often worth comparatively little or nothing compared to a nice clean copy. Booksellers are duty-bound by a self-imposed rule to mention that a book is from a library.

One other thing you may not know but of which you should be aware is that Book-of-the-Month-Club (or any book club) copies, while putatively "first editions" by reason of their date and other points are in fact virtually worthless. People bring in "firsts" of Hemingway's The Old Man and the Sea all the time, with dust jackets, in Book-of-the Month Club editions, and we have to tell them it's a £15 book.

Charlie

*

From: L.Dickerson@verizon.net
To: Charlie.Dover@duquest.co.uk
September 9, 2012

Dear Charlie

Thanks on all the library business.

Book clubs. <u>Now</u> you tell me: I fell for a Book-of-the-Month Club <u>Catcher in the Rye</u>. But it was only $230. I also fell for an early edition with a "facsimile" dust jacket for $500. Doubtless that was a mistake, too. But they are conversation pieces. A really good copy with very fine jacket of <u>Catcher</u> would break my book budget.

Larry

CHAPTER ELEVEN

From: L.Dickerson@verizon.net
To: Irving.Gross@ns.edu
September 9, 2012

Dear Irving

I told you how I had finished that huge Library of America Thurber, and had picked up a few inexpensive cartoon books of his, and was about to start on The Years with Ross. Just then the name Salinger came up, and we were both off like crazy on Salinger and that led to Lolita and Nabokov.

I like Thurber's The Years with Ross best of all his writings. I have read through the latest modern version (the one with the introduction by the New Yorker writer Adam Gopnik). I think, and this may be a sad confession on my part, that it is the funniest book I have ever read. It "kills me, and all," as Holden Caulfield would say. As you know, Thurber was blind by the time he wrote his book on Ross and couldn't do any more cartoons. I see that he published about 25 books. But I don't see (from reading that huge Library of American collection), how the rest of his prose, good as it is, comes up to The Years with Ross. I have my eye on a "flat-signed" copy at $700.

Larry

And how about The New Yorker's guidelines for editing fiction, printed in Thurber's Ross book? I suppose most of them would apply to any writing. For instance, they say that if you think something may be a cliche it probably is. Good rule, eh? Another rule is not allowing foreign phrases if there is a good English equivalent. I myself am almost tempted sometimes to use n'est ce pas – except that I am not sure how to spell it and have to look it up every time. So I stick with "Right?" or "Yes?" Listen to me, talking shop with an English professor. Coals to Newcastle.

From: Irving.Gross@ns.edu
To: L.Dickerson@verizon.net
September 10, 2012

Dear Larry

The Years with Ross is indeed a funny book. I remember the part in the
book about how in 1940, at the time of the London Blitz, Ross went to
visit Thurber in the hospital where he was having an eye operation, and
Ross told him, "Thurber, I worry about you and England." And the account
of Thurber and Ross visiting Paris after the War, when Ross wouldn't get
out of the taxi to see Notre Dame, just stopped for a moment to look out
of the window and say that the building had never been sandblasted. He
refused to go to see the Sainte Chapelle stained glass windows, saying,
"Stained glass is damned embarrassing." I wonder just what he meant by
that. And he wouldn't go into the Louvre. "They've only got three things
worth seeing in there, and I've seen color reproductions of them all."

Clichés. Yes, that is a good rule of thumb.

Foreign languages, right. But sometimes there is nothing quite like, say, the
French au fond – so much better than "basically" (literally "at bottom").

Yours
Irving

From: L.Dickerson@verizon.net
To: Irving.Gross@ns.edu
September 10, 2012

Dear Irving

    Basically, I don't see that <u>au fond</u> is any better than "basically" or "at bottom."

                          Larry

*   *   *

From: smeans101@aol.com
To: Irving.Gross@ns.edu
September 12, 2012

Dear Irving

    How is teaching going this new term? Still have them reading books, I hope, not just criticism?
    Our by now mutual friend, Larry Dickerson, has been up here again since broadening into <u>New Yorker</u> writers, and he tells me he thinks <u>The Years With Ross</u> the funniest book he has ever read (and he's half way through re-reading it). A bit of a stretch, but then it's hard to stay funny on the page over the years, and Thurber does it as well as anyone. And of course Thurber had a great subject in the eccentric Harold Ross.

                          Spencer

My favorite line from that book is when a cartoonist at the magazine asks Ross, "Why do you reject drawings of mine and print stuff by that fifth-rate artist Thurber?" To which Ross snaps back, "You mean third-rate."

*

From: Irving.Gross@ns.edu
To: smeans101@aol.com
September 14, 2012

Dear Spencer

Yes, Dickerson does indeed love the Thurber book on Ross. Over the phone Larry asked if there were any connection between Bobbie Ross of Oscar Wilde fame and Harold Ross of The New Yorker: "I knew damn well that they very probably weren't related, but I was just checking to make sure so I don't go and make a damn fool of myself." He added, "I recently learned that the English painter Lucian Freud was the grandson of Freud himself. So you never know, do you?" I can't help but admire a person so unashamedly frank and humbly inquisitive, not at all afraid to "make sure he has things straight."

What did Dickerson think of your Thurber drawings?

Irving

*

From: smeans101@aol.com
To: Irving.Gross@ns.edu
September 17, 2012

Dear Irving

When Dickerson came up here for a second time, he was like a kid in a candy shop. He especially loved the Thurber drawings. He says that it must be great to own a drawing by someone with a big name and whom "you actually like." I suspect that he, if asked, would honestly say he didn't like, for example, my little Miro pencil drawing. But a Thurber figurative cartoon of a dog lights him up.

In a further development, when I told him I had a doctor's

appointment on East 14th Street the following Wednesday, he as much as insisted I come by his place afterwards to see his growing collection. I did. I'm afraid he needs more direction. Of course, I could not bring myself to say anything like that. I hadn't the heart to tell him that he must learn to pay more attention to the condition of the books he buys. On the other hand, his Victorian books include five or six with signatures. Very impressive. He got three of them from a dealer I know only by name, Phillip Osgood. Larry's Victorian titles are chiefly in rebound copies, and that's fine for his level of collecting. However, there is plenty of foxing, bumps, slightly cocked spines and other defects detrimental to the book's value. His New Yorker collection, though far from perfect, is better, but even there he has a Book-of-the-Month Club Catcher in the Rye and another with a facsimile jacket.

Of course you are not a collector yourself, but I'm sure you understand these matters.

Spencer

* * *

From: L.Dickerson@verizon.net
To: Charlie.Dover@duquest.co.uk
September 18, 2012

Dear Charlie

Please take a look at this email forwarded to me from Gross, an email he got from Spencer Means, the collector he introduced me to. I don't know if he sent it to me by mistake or on purpose. It's very discouraging. So, I'm "a kid in a candy shop" — well maybe I am. But what he says about my Victorian books is a little scary. Not that I am going to try to recoup my money. I know it's way too late to even think of that. But I can't help but be a little annoyed at both of them. Any advice for your old friend?

Larry

*

From: Charlie.Dover@duquest.co.co.uk
To: L.Dickerson@verizon.net
19 September 2012

Dear Larry

I do have some advice for you, and I feel very keenly that I am right: forget it. You yourself are always talking about your being "old," and it's simply the case that most senior people don't have too many friends, and don't make too many new ones. You don't want to lose the friends you have. I would just ignore this email. All right, so you have made some mistakes, especially as regards condition. (And those worthless early Trollopes, and that three-decker you told me about.) Spencer Means is obviously a pro, and a man of means (I knew you'd like that). But what was he going to tell you? That most of your Victorian copies are in less than good condition? That he said it to your other book friend and adviser, Irving Gross, should remain in confidence. Both men would be upset if they knew about this. Forget the whole business is my strong advice.

Charlie

*

From: L.Dickerson@verizon.net
To: Charlie.Dover@duquest.co.uk
September 19, 2012

So you don't think Gross sent it on to me on purpose?

*

107

From: Charlie.Dover@duquest.co.uk
To: L.Dickerson@verizon.net
20 September 2012

Dear Larry

Not only do I not think so, I feel that even if he did forward the email to you deliberately, the part about imperfections in your collected books is something it won't hurt you to know.

Don't even think about jeopardizing two friendships over this. None of us wants to know what our friends say about us to third parties. If it weren't so grand to say so, I'd insist that not knowing what our friends think about us is part of our social contract.

Charlie

*

From: L.Dickerson@verizon.net
To: Charlie.Dover@duquest.co.uk
September 20, 2012

Dear Charlie

   You're right of course. It just hurt my pride a little. On the other hand, I must be more careful about condition. But on the other other hand, if I were to have bought the kind of superb-condition books Spencer Means likes, I would only have about three Victorian books for my entire $25,000.

Larry

* * *

From: Irving.Gross@ns.edu
To: smeans101@aol.com
September 22, 2012

Dear Spencer

I can see how you didn't want to warn Larry to be more condition-conscious in his book buying. He's enjoying the "chase," as he calls it, so much so that it wouldn't do to criticize his purchases. God knows he is honest enough to admit his mistakes, but it's not your duty, nor mine, to fault his past purchases.

Now that I have been re-reading Thurber's classic The Years with Ross, I begin to see something. My idea is that Larry Dickerson is, mutatis mutandis, rather like Harold Ross himself. Naturally, no one is going to claim Dickerson is a "genius in disguise." On the other hand, there are striking similarities and not all of them obvious ones. Bear with me:

Like Ross, Dickerson is uneducated, but eager to learn; he freely admits he doesn't know a lot of things, things that maybe he should know, especially things people know if they went to college and were "English majors." Recall that Ross wasn't afraid to ask, "Is Moby Dick the whale or the guy?" or to scribble, "Who he?" next to the name of William Blake, or his memorable query to the phrase, "the woman taken in adultery": "Who is this? not mentioned earlier." (Recall Oscar Wilde saying that some friend "was always conducting his education in public.")

Girl-shy Ross was squeamish about sex. On hearing any "bathroom or bedroom stuff," he would say, "I don't want to hear about it." From what I can tell, Dickerson, a shy person and especially shy with women, is easily imagined as saying similar things.

Ross and Dickerson both have rather literal minds.

Dickerson's insistence that words have pretty much one standard, constant, "correct" meaning is distinctly Rossian.

Dickerson is a sloppy dresser. Ross was famously a terrible dresser.

Both use vulgar and profane language, of which neither seems conscious. Ross continuously used "Goddam" and "Jesus." Recall Ross telling an illustrator, "Jee-sus — that's not an admiral, it's a goddam doorman." Dickerson, I am convinced, really doesn't try to be tough-sounding or vulgar; he just says "goddam nice" where other people would say "very nice." His "Jaysus" and "Christ" are the equivalent of "What?" or "Granted." Ross, sometimes, after a lot of back and forth on some particular problem, would shove the matter aside and say, "The hell with it." I have heard Dickerson react similarly to certain apparently unsolvable problems, such as why there is something, the universe, rather than nothing. (This last seems, oddly enough, to be a real concern of Larry's.)

Both are worriers, and especially about money, or "dough." (Dickerson keeps me and his Christie's lady friend up to date on his "Financial outlay.")

Both are obsessive.

Both are workaholics.

Both delight in exaggeration, by way of highlighting a conviction or prejudice; Ross telling Peter Arno, "I think you are the greatest artist in the world." Ditto for Dickerson, insisting that Vanity Fair is the greatest novel ever written, easily topping War and Peace, not to mention Ulysses.

Ross had a penchant for comic funny stories over "grim" ones: "If a man in these goddam New Yorker stories doesn't shoot his wife, he shoots himself. Everybody gets into bed with everybody else. It's a hell of a thing but I guess there's nothing to do about it." Larry too usually retreats from "grim" stories and can't understand just why he should like Tess of the D'Urbervilles as much as he does.

Both are given to crude generalizations; Ross, for example, announced with finality, "All Communists had unhappy childhoods."

Ross viewed modern abstract art "disconsolately" – as does Dickerson: "You don't know if these abstract artists can even draw."

Ross preferred slang terms, "the bughouse," "dough," "the dope on something," and so does our man.

Both delight in odd or unusual facts

Ross got along well with cops. I don't know about Larry, but I wouldn't be surprised.

And, come to think of it, Dickerson is even an editor, of his great great grandfather's correspondence.

Of course one can't go too far with this: Ross was, additionally, a visionary, an innovator, a genius of an editor, a pioneer, the founder and spirit behind The New Yorker. His legacy exists right down to today, more than sixty years after his death.

Sorry for the length. But I find Larry a beguiling and interesting man.

Just a thought.

Irving

*

From: smeans101@aol.com
To: Irving.Gross@ns.edu
September 22, 2012

Dear Irving

It's an interesting thought. And a meandering one. Have him read Brendan Gill as partial antidote to his admiration for Ross.

Spencer

* * *

From: Irving.Gross@ns.edu
To: L.Dickerson@verizon.net
September 23, 2012

Dear Larry

Since you are so delighted with Thurber's portrait of Harold Ross, you must read the other history of The New Yorker by another first-rate writer and contributor to the magazine, Brendan Gill. He started at The New Yorker as a very young man in 1936 and wrote for it until he died in 1997. That's 61 years. He wrote fifteen books but only one that truly endures, Here at The New Yorker, 1975. Much of the book is given to contrasting Ross, editor for the first 26 years, and William Shawn, still editor after 24 years when Gill wrote his book. It's more than plain that Gill disliked Ross and thought him over-rated, whereas he venerated Shawn.

We learn that Ross's voice was loud, rasping, and Western; Shawn's is soft, rounded, and standard American. Ross spoke Billingsgate; the harshest expletive ever heard from Shawn was a whispered, "Oh God!" As for manners, "Ross might truly be said not to have had any," whereas Shawn has never been known to go through a door ahead of a companion. Both Ross and Shawn were energetic, Ross in a loud aggressive way, Shawn in a quiet determined way. Both were puritanical, but Shawn would never have uttered Ross's crude warning to his editors, "Don't fuck the contributors." Beyond this, Gill saw Ross as "lamentably" uninformed in matters sexual, such as his going around after his child was born a girl and saying, "I don't like the idea of having all these female hormones in me." On the other hand, Shawn, while remaining married, had a long standing affair with New Yorker colleague Lillian Ross, his "second wife" of forty years. Ross's mistress was the New Yorker.

However, in spite of everything Gill has to say, I myself prefer Thurber's version of Ross – the negatives are there but somehow redeemed by humor. I'm sure you will, too. But you should read Gill.

Irving

From: L.Dickerson@verizon.net
To: Irving.Gross@ns.edu
September 24, 2012

Irving

I phoned the Strand and they are holding a copy of Gill's Here at The New Yorker for me, although you told me so much that I almost don't need to read the book.

Larry

113

CHAPTER TWELVE

From: L.Dickerson@verizon.net
To: Irving.Gross@ns.edu
September 28, 2012

Dear Irving

OK, I am leaving in abeyance Thurber's 25 books to collect other things, although I did eventually get that first edition of The Years with Ross "flat-signed" for $700 – ordinary copies go for $300 down to $100. I'd love to get a few original Thurber cartoons.

I like it when "my" New Yorker authors interact, even when they interact nastily. I see in Slawenski that Mary McCarthy was very critical of Franny and Zooey. She said that Salinger, like Hemingway, has characters divided into allies and enemies, those who belong to the club and those who don't. She also says, "And who are these wonder Glass kids but Salinger himself?" Still, I want to read and get at least one of her books – a high point. Which do you recommend?

Larry

Total outlay to date: $27,100.

But see how here my $700 splurge on a signed Years with Ross is nothing like the $4,200 for Tess of the D'Urbervilles. Except for Catcher in the Rye and Lolita, my new focus writers are quite inexpensive compared to the Victorians. Which is probably as it ought to be.

*

From: Irving.Gross@ns.edu
To: L.Dickerson@verizon.net
September 28, 2012

Dear Larry

Mary McCarthy's best book, hands down, is <u>Memories of a Catholic Girlhood</u>. One reviewer of the book wrote that McCarthy "writes better than most people and here she writes better than herself." It originally appeared in installments in <u>The New Yorker</u>, so the book fits nicely into your collecting program.

Irving

Here's an early version of McCarthy's famous "stare."

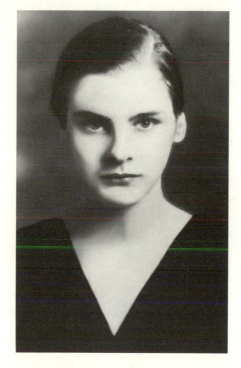

*

From: L.Dickerson@verizon.net
To: Irving.Gross@ns.edu
September 30, 2012

Dear Irving

    Ok. I have read in paperback McCarthy's <u>Memories of a Catholic Girlhood</u>. I think the chapter called "The Tin Butterfly" is worth the price of admission. So is the chapter about the priest's sermon at her school having everyone worry that her nice grandfather would go to hell because he was a Protestant. And the part about her losing her faith and <u>announcing</u> this to the nuns. Beautiful.
    And that's quite a stare.
    Beyond <u>Memories</u>, I don't think I want to collect Mary McCarthy; partly because she disliked Salinger's work – or at least the Glass family stuff. But I understand that this is silly on my part. Still, there it is.
    Another amazing thing I've learned about <u>Memories of a Catholic Girlhood</u> is that when it appeared in installments in <u>The New Yorker</u> many readers thought they were fiction – not autobiography.

                                                    Larry

                              *

From: Irving.Gross@ns.edu
To: L.Dickerson@verizon.net
October 2, 2012

Dear Larry

In regards to readers thinking the <u>Memories</u> installments were fictional: in fact they <u>are</u> largely fictional. As are all the stories we tell about ourselves (beyond dates and names). There are academics who say that all fiction is autobiographical, and others who say that all autobiography is fiction. Some critics go so far as to say that any book with an author's name on

the title page is autobiography; still others say a writer's true
autobiography can come out only symbolically in the writer's fiction or
poetry. The layman's common-sense view that some fictions are more
autobiographical than others and that some autobiographies are more
fictional than others appeals to me, but we won't settle that question here.

Irving

PS McCarthy got into a famous feud with Lillian Hellman. On a PBS TV
interview, Dick Cavett asked McCarthy to name writers she considered
over-rated. She said Pearl Buck, John Steinbeck, and Lillian Hellman. "Why
Hellman?" asked Cavett. And McCarthy said, "Because every word she
writes is a lie, including 'and' and 'the'." Hellman went to the law over it.
After five years she died before the case came to court.

*

From: L.Dickerson@verizon.net
To: Irving.Gross@ns.edu
October 3, 2012

Dear Irving

    Far be it for me to try to even enter into the argument about fiction
being autobiographical and autobiographies being fictional. But I see a
"very good" copy of Memories with dust jacket at $400. I'll get that one
and then move on (or move back to, I should say) Updike, who is
mentioned in the same paragraph of Slawenski as being disappointed with
Franny and Zooey. I haven't done anything on Updike.

Larry

Total outlay to date: $27,500.

CHAPTER THIRTEEN

From: Irving.Gross@ns.edu
To: L.Dickerson@verizon.net
October 6, 2012

Dear Larry

Updike began his writing for The New Yorker in the 1950s and continued sending them short stories regularly; one story was in the works and appeared after his death. In all he is said to have supplied the magazine with some 800 pieces, short stories, poems, memoirs, reviews, etc. He has been called "E. B. White on steroids."

One Updike-hater asked, "Has the son of a bitch ever had one unpublished thought?" Saul Bellow in a recently published private letter called him an "anti-Semitic pornographer." The anti-Semitic thing is baseless, not worthy of rebuttal, take the word of a Jew for it. "Pornographer" – well, yes, Updike is probably the most sexually explicit of any respected novelist. If that's what you mean by pornography.

Irving

By the way, here is something you will find more interesting than I do. In 1960 Updike published a piece called "Hub Fans Bid Kid Adieu" in The New Yorker, an account of Ted Williams' last at bat ever. The Boston fans are praying, beseeching the baseball gods for you know what. Well, sure enough, Williams hits a home run. Story-book ending to a long career. The crowd cheers and begs (even the umpires beg) him to come out of the dugout and take a bow, but he won't do it. He never had, and he wasn't going to do so on this day, either. I've heard Updike's piece called the finest example of baseball reporting ever written. But I am no judge.

*

From: L.Dickerson@verizon.net
To: Irving.Gross@ns.edu
October 7, 2012

Dear Irving

Of course I'll search out the baseball story.

I'd love to have the four Rabbit books, but I take it they would push me way over my budget. And of course these were books that didn't appear in The New Yorker. Perhaps I should begin by reading and then collecting his early short stories from The New Yorker. I see Updike once told an interviewer that seeing his first story in print in The New Yorker was the most "ecstatic" moment in his sixty years of professional writing.

Larry

*

From: Irving.Gross@ns.edu
To: L.Dickerson@verizon.net
October 8, 2012

Dear Larry

There is also "Rabbit Remembered," a short piece – a kind of coda – to the whole Rabbit quartet. It is part of a collection called Licks of Love. You can pick it up for a song, as they say.

Updike is disliked by many feminists; he's a Great Male Narcissist, "just a penis with a thesaurus." His spectacular prose is used against him by his detractors as too brilliant, too attention-calling; too preeningly male, etc. Myself, I think he will outlast his detractors.

119

Incidentally, do you remember that conversation we had about the problem of why the world exists — the universe rather than nothing? I've just read a whole book on the subject, by Jim Holt, and he quotes Updike as telling him that the question is just too much for us, as if we expected a dog to understand how they invented the internal-combustion engine.

Updike died without getting the Nobel Prize for literature, which in my view was a disgrace. For all Bellow's genius, I prefer the all-too-prolific Updike. I suspect that for many years he came up just short in the Nobel judging. And of course, with Toni Morrison the committee selected a black writer, a woman, and an American. Well, fine. I can see that. Some people unfairly look upon Morrison as a kind of affirmative-action Nobel Prize winner. But it's largely become that in any event. The fact is they don't want to give too many awards to the same country, and after hers and before that Bellow's, there was no room for another American. The Nobel prizes are a pet peeve of mine. Why, for instance, did Edward O. Wilson never get one in biology? Don't get me started.

Irving

*

From: L.Dickerson@verizon.net
To: Irving.Gross@ns.edu
October 10, 2012

Dear Irving,

    Having never heard of Edward O. Wilson, it sure beats me why he didn't get a Nobel.
    Updike's "Hub Fans Bid Kid Adieu" is the best baseball article imaginable. Certainly the best I've ever read — and I've read thousands of them.

Larry

Maybe Updike's comment on why the world exists is simply a more polite way of saying – as I do of such a question – the hell with it.

*

From: Irving.Gross@ns.edu
To: L.Dickerson@verizon.net
October 10, 2012

Never heard of Edward O. Wilson? And you call yourself a Darwinian?

*

From: L.Dickerson@verizon.net
To: Irving.Gross@ns.edu
October 12, 2012

Hey, I asked a man who lives in my building, and who teaches high school science, about Edward O. Wilson not getting a Nobel Prize, and he said there is no Nobel prize for biology, only physiology or medicine, but not biology.

                                              Larry

*

From: Irving.Gross@ns.edu
To: L.Dickerson@verizon.net
October 12, 2012

Larry

Thanks on no Nobel Prize for biology. We live and learn, as you say.

I highly recommend you get Updike's <u>Self-Consciousness</u>, autobiographical fragments that first appeared in <u>The New Yorker</u>.

Yes, you might read and maybe collect Updike's first collection of <u>New Yorker</u> stories, <u>The Same Door</u>.

Irving

*

From: L.Dickerson@verizon.net
To: Irving.Gross@ns.edu
October 13, 2012

Dear Irving

   <u>Self-Consciousness</u> is so inexpensive I'm getting a first edition on your recommendation without first reading it. How is that for trust?
   I've ordered <u>The Same Door</u> for $300. My guess is that Updike signed many copies of his books — so many that for later books the signed price is pretty low.
   I'm rereading parts of the <u>Rabbit</u> books. But reading has competition with football these weekends. I waste many hours of my life looking at sports. Christ, when I think of how many hours I spent watching the goddam London Olympics last August. Even archery, for God's sake. As for buying these <u>Rabbit</u> books, I see I can get a set of all four in first editions, signed, for $4,500. Sounds like a huge amount of money in one

122

shot, but since it's four books, they come to only $1,125 each. I say "only." They would mean goodbye to my revised budget of $30,000

Larry

*

From: Irving.Gross@ns.edu
To: L.Dickerson@verizon.net
October 13, 2012

Dear Larry

I'm deeply touched that on my recommendation you would buy a first edition of Updike's <u>Self-Consciousness</u> before reading it. As for signed Updike books, ask Spencer. He may have some stories.

Irving

*   *   *

From: L.Dickerson@verizon.net
To: smeans101@aol.com
October 22, 2012

Dear Spencer

   I am well into collecting <u>New Yorker</u> writers. I have been getting some inscribed or signed copies, most notably just now by John Updike. Irving says you may know something special about inscribed copies?

Larry

*

123

From: smeans101@aol.com
To: L. Dickerson@verizon.net
October 22, 2012

Dear Larry

    As you may know I was a good friend of the late Nathan Halderin. Halderin was close friends with a professor named John Harrington, who ran a literary lecture series at a college in New Jersey. This fellow used to "hire" Halderin, who lived in NYC, to drive eminent visiting lecturers to the college campus; Harrington figuring, quite correctly, that Halderin would enjoy meeting writers like Tom Stoppard, Mary McCarthy, Elizabeth Hardwicke, Ted Hughes, and John Updike. What struck Halderin about Updike was his almost saint-like patience after his talk, signing for what seemed like hours, what must have been many hundreds of copies of his books. Halderin said he remembers hearing each petitioner asking Updike something like, "Would you make it 'For Sarah,' – that's Sarah with an 'h'?"
    Halderin told me that in his car – a Toyota Corolla – he asked Updike if he himself owned a Toyota. Updike said No, but that he had visited a Toyota dealership while writing Rabbit is Rich, in which, as you know, Rabbit has inherited his father-in-law's Toyota dealership. Halderin then asked Updike for his views on Trollope. Updike got no further than saying, "Of course I took the title Rabbit Redux from Trollope..." when he was interrupted. John Harrington was hard of hearing, and from the back seat, fearing the conversation was flagging, interrupted and asked, "Mr. Updike, did you have a pleasant flight down from Boston?" Trollope didn't come up again. Halderin, whose chief interest was Trollope, never forgave Harrington.

                                                        Spencer

                                    *

From: L.Dickerson@verizon.net
To: smeans101@aol.com
October 23, 2012

Dear Spencer

   Thanks for those stories. I went uptown yesterday to buy a set of four
Rabbit books, signed first editions. $4,500. What do you think?

                                                    Larry

                                *

From: smeans101@aol.com
To: L.Dickerson@verizon.net
October 23, 2012

   Sounds fairly steep. And their condition?

                                *

From: L.Dickerson@verizon.net
To: smeans101@aol.com
October 25, 2012

Dear Spencer

   I bet you will be proud to hear that despite having my heart set on
those Rabbit books, I have returned them (I had seven days). Closer
examination, partly inspired by your question, showed various small faults,
a few underlinings, pages bent back, etc. Condition, condition, condition.
I also thought they were overpriced, whatever their condition. Maybe I'll
content myself with collecting Updike's first New Yorker collected short
stories – The Same Door. Those Rabbit books would have pushed me
way over my budget. I must learn to be less impulsive.

                                125

My highest single outlay remains $4,200 for Tess of the D'Urbervilles, three volumes, in nice full leather bindings. I fear I overpaid there. I have seen copies in allegedly "very good" condition for $2,200. It will kill me if I see a nice signed copy for $3,000.

Larry

*

From: smeans101@aol.com
To: L.Dickerson@verizon.net
October 25, 2012

Dear Larry

My advice is: Don't look at any more prices for Tess. What's done is done. It's way too late to return the book, and you wouldn't get near your value if you tried to sell it now. You win some, you lose some, the old cliché. All book collectors have been through it.

Spencer

* * *

From: Irving.Gross@ns.edu
To: L.Dickerson@verizon.net
November 4, 2012

Dear Larry

I see you've done nothing in regard to E.B. White — considered by many the greatest asset Ross had from the early days at The New Yorker (and during later years, too). White did a good deal of everything — writing pieces, editing, doing "Talk of the Town," and originating the famous

"Newsbreaks": for example, under the heading "We Don't Want To Hear About It," the magazine would print misprints or ambiguous lines from other publications, such as "…the fish with three girls instead of two…" White also "tinkered" with or supplied many of the legends to the cartoons, the most famous being the drawing showing a mother talking to her four-year-old daughter at table: "It's broccoli, dear," to which the child answers, "I say it's spinach and I say the hell with it."

Irving

*

From: L.Dickerson@verizon.net
To: Irving.Gross@ns.edu
November 5, 2012

Dear Irving

    I'm not going to bother with collecting E. B. White. All the books say he was a great New Yorker writer and stylist, but I see his best known books are children's books, Stuart Little and Charlotte's Web. I'm not going to start collecting children's stories. Call it a prejudice, if you want. Call it broccoli, if you want.
    I read that White was a very shy man. He would go out on the fire escape of his office rather than meet strangers being shown around.

Larry

*

From: Irving.Gross@ns.edu
To: L.Dickerson@verizon.net
November 7, 2012

Dear Larry

OK, but I do recommend to you a small book of White's. It's called <u>The Elements of Style</u> and is an update of a little private textbook by William Strunk, who was White's English professor at Cornell. It's only about 70 pages, and you need not read it end to end. For forty or so years almost every college Introduction to English Composition course either used the book (it sold millions) or was taught by a man or woman who had imbibed it. I had the book assigned to me at college, and I in turn have assigned or recommended it to my students.

"Strunk and White," as the book came to be called, advocates a simple, direct writing style. Now, Larry, you read so much and write so many emails about writers that I think you would enjoy poking around in this little book. I don't mean to say that elaborate writers (Faulkner, Nabokov) are not admirable; it's just that for most of us non-geniuses it's best to write in plain English. Today, <u>The Elements of Style</u> is sometimes frowned upon by those who consider it too "prescriptive," too "apodictic" (a word Strunk & White would have objected to), and too insistent on correct usage, too "elitist." But it still has plenty to offer anyone interested in the craft of writing. I can remember a handful of their strictures and commands. For example,

<u>Use the active voice</u>: not "My visit to Boston will always be remembered by me," but "I will always remember my visit to Boston."

<u>Use "There is" and "There are" only sparingly</u>: they can usually be omitted.

<u>Use "definite, specific, concrete" language</u>: not "A period of unfavorable weather set in," but "It rained every day for two weeks."

<u>Place emphatic words last (or, more rarely, first)</u>: "Home is the sailor."

On the other hand, you can see how old fashioned it is to write things like "There is no such word as alright."

Irving

From: L.Dickerson@verizon.net
To: Irving.Gross@ns.edu
November 10, 2012

Dear Irving

   "Alright," but what a fascinating little book! (Cost, $7.) And there I go breaking two rules already – over-use of "little" and using the exclamation mark for emphasis.
   Strunk & White say "interesting" is an "unconvincing word." It's interesting to know that. They sort out "farther" and "further"; and "like" and "as." They also clear up "imply" and "infer"; and "lie" and "lay," and "less" and "fewer," etc.
   I like it when they say that "-wise" is not to be used "indiscriminately" as a "pseudosuffix," as in, "The car was pricewise a bargain." Jaysus, the ridiculous overuse of "-wise" is if anything more alive today nearly a century after Strunk had White as a student in class. Timewise, the "pseudosuffix" is thriving.
   I was delighted to hear them say "Avoid foreign languages."
   But what I like most is that they say that "enormity" means "monstrous wickedness," not "bigness."

                               Larry

And how about their point about not explaining too much, especially with "-ly" adverbs, as in "… she said grumblingly."

From: Irving.Gross@ns.edu
To: L.Dickerson@verizon.net
November 13, 2012

Dear Larry

There's a legend (note the Struck & White violation) that in 1920s Paris, Gertrude Stein told the young Ernest Hemingway to write with nouns and verbs, not adjectives and adverbs. In any event, Hemingway's sparse style had an enormous influence among American writers (and college-aged, would-be writers). Strunk and White use that very formula, "Write with nouns and verbs" (an injunction in the original Strunk booklet well before the time of Stein and Hemingway).

On a curious but germane note, Gabriel García Márquez says in his autobiography that as a young newspaperman, he determined to avoid the "bankrupt habit" of using -mente adverbs, the English equivalent, "-ly": for example, he would never employ felizmente, "happily," or renuentemente, "reluctantly." He says that he doesn't know if his translators have acquired his "stylistic paranoia" about -mente adverbs. I once had the good fortune of meeting Gregory Rabassa, English translator of One Hundred Years of Solitude. When asked about García Márquez's avoidance of this adverbial form, Rabassa replied, simply, "That's right." I have asked students and friends who were reading that great novel whether they could discover an "-ly" adverb in the English translation. So far, none has turned up.

Irving

I'm not saying we should follow García Márquez's paranoia. I for one don't see anything wrong with "-ly" adverbs in English. It's just that you don't want too many of them and certainly not two in a row. "He looked lovingly hopefully into her eyes." This offhand example reminds me that for years English professors inveighed in vain against the word "hopefully."

I used to tell my freshman class that if any student could use the word properly in a sentence (or in what I then conceived of as the only proper use of the adverb), we would call the class short on the spot. Never once did I have to dismiss the class early. I got sentences like "It won't rain hopefully tomorrow," or "We will win the game hopefully next time."

*

From: L.Dickerson@verizon.net
To: Irving.Gross@ns.edu
November 13, 2012

Dear Irving

Hopefully, I won't misuse the word when writing to you.

Larry

CHAPTER FOURTEEN

From: L.Dickerson@verizon.net
To: Irving.Gross@ns.edu
November 14, 2012

Dear Irving

    Me again. Enough on style and words. Everybody in books about The New Yorker – Thurber, Gill, Kunkel, Yagoda – raves about Joseph Mitchell's writings. Can you tell me why, before I start reading, much less collecting him?

Larry

*

From: Irving.Gross@ns.edu
To: L.Dickerson@verizon.net
November 16, 2012

Dear Larry

I can't really tell you why I also think Mitchell is one of America's foremost prose writers. This kind of judgment is entirely subjective. But when you find many people sharing the same opinion, it's time to sit up and pay attention. So, in 1992 when Mitchell collected all four of his New Yorker books into one, called Up in the Old Hotel, it was a great hit. I copy out for you some of the blurbs from the paperback:

"Mitchell's darkly comic articles are models of big-city journalism. His accounts are what Joyce might have written had he gone into journalism." Newsweek.

"A poetry of the actual, a song of the street that casts a wide net and fearlessly embraces everything human....This is reporting transformed into literature." San Francisco Chronicle.

"Up in the Old Hotel makes the case for journalism as literature about as well as it can be made." Newsday.

So just read him and see what you think.

This may come as a surprise to you but Mitchell lived in the same building as I still do; he lived here before I got here (in the late 1980s) and died here in 1996. I even have an inscribed copy of Up in the Old Hotel, but unfortunately it's not inscribed to me. Mitchell gave this inscribed copy to Mrs. Holland who lived here forever – as did Mitchell. (Her heirs must have sold it to the Strand Bookstore because I found it there on the open shelves.) I used to pass Joe Mitchell in the lobby and ride with him in the elevator. We would nod and say hello. He was always dressed perfectly; even in summer he would wear a fedora and a light seersucker suit and have a slim briefcase tucked under his arm. He was supremely polite but there was something about him that said, Don't come too close or engage me in conversation.

His four New Yorker books were McSorley's Wonderful Saloon; Old Mr. Flood; The Bottom of the Harbor; and Joe Gould's Secret, this last coming out in 1965.

Now, as everybody concerned knows so well, after 1965 Mitchell never published anything. He was on the staff at The New Yorker; he had his own office, and he went to it every day, and he got paid. During those last years everybody – not least the New Yorker editors – was hoping and praying that he was about to come out with another marvelous profile or investigative piece, but he never did. One New Yorker writer remembers coming down in the elevator with him at the close of work one day and hearing him give out a rather sad sigh. It was a case of writer's block as severe as any. Salinger, we are given to believe, actually wrote daily during his years of seclusion; he just wouldn't publish anything. But Mitchell apparently left nothing behind.

133

For all my admiration for Mitchell, I see a problem with his wonderful stories. (Although, speaking of wonderful, McSorley's Saloon is still there, on East 7th Street and quite the same as when Mitchell described it in 1940.) I think that reportage pieces, no matter how glorious, <u>date</u> in the sense that we know things are different now; we know that these real people whom he admired and chronicled are gone: saloon keepers, seamen, lobstermen, gypsy fortune tellers, Mohawk Indian high steel workers, street preachers, a bearded lady – the odder citizens of the city. And journalism, no matter how brilliant, can't live the way fiction does. Fictional characters are still doing, thinking, acting. David Copperfield is still running away from Murdstone and Grimsby; Holden Caulfield is still wearing his red hunting hat in inappropriate places and asking the cab driver if he happens to know where the ducks go when their pond in Central Park freezes over. But the gypsy woman's clever cons in 1938, though factual, are in a real sense gone. She is stuck in 1938. Mitchell's writing may be the best of its kind <u>ever</u>, but – well, it's not like the staleness of last week's newspaper, he's too good for that – one cannot help feeling that this material inevitably has not the life that it had when the pieces were published between 1938 and 1965. How could it?

It is no surprise that Mitchell was a favorite of Ross, who shared with Mitchell an absolute obsession with facts, especially strange facts. That's why Ross (although he complained of how slow Mitchell was) kept him on, always in hope that sometime soon Mitchell would be forthcoming. The hope was shared by Ross's successor, William Shawn, and in turn by Robert Gottlieb and Tina Brown. After Mitchell's death, there was a hope that some hidden manuscript would come to light via his estate. None came. One theory is that Mitchell worked with and wrote about the Greenwich Village street character Joe Gould for too long a time. Mitchell met Gould in the late 1930s, published his first profile of him in 1942, and the second and final profile in 1964. Joe Gould's "secret" was that his huge Oral History, the project he kept telling Mitchell about, didn't exist. Gould was a blocked would-be writer, and some think that Mitchell identified with Gould, and ended up a sort of Joe Gould himself, after the second of his profiles on Gould was published.

134

I'm putting this signed Mitchell book into the mail for you.

Irving

*

From: L.Dickerson@verizon.net
To: Irving.Gross@ns.edu
November 18, 2012

Dear Irving

   That's really so kind of you to send me that autographed copy of Up in the Old Hotel. I know you are not a collector, and even though it was not inscribed to you – still. Many, many thanks.
   I write some long emails – but I think you are beginning to take the cake. I'm not complaining, simply observing. Many thanks for all the dope on Mitchell.
   It is not hard to find all four of his books. Mitchell's last and most famous book, Joe Gould's Secret, can be picked up inscribed for $4,500! And a decent unsigned copy goes for $1,000. Christ, this by itself shows how highly regarded Mitchell was, or is. And how expensive authors' inscriptions can be.
   I find in one of his pieces from 1938 Mitchell claims that his greatest achievement happened the year before when he came in third in a clam-eating contest on Long Island – he ate 84 cherrystones.

Larry

*

From: Irving.Gross@ns.edu
To: L.Dickerson@verizon.net
November 18, 2012

Dear Larry

I myself like best Mitchell's line to someone who asked him if all the
famous <u>New Yorker</u> writers had something in common, something that
made them "<u>New Yorker</u> writers." "Well," he replied with that easy
Southern drawl, "None of 'em could spell."

Irving

                              *

From: L.Dickerson@verizon.net
To: Irving.Gross@ns.edu
November 20, 2012

Dear Irving

    Reading around in books about <u>The New Yorker</u> I also find nothing but
good said about A.J. Liebling. He was immensely prolific, unlike his great
friend and your favorite, Joseph Mitchell. How about Liebling?

                                              Larry

                              *

From: Irving.Gross@ns.edu
To: L.Dickerson@verizon.net
November 21, 2012

Dear Larry

You're right. I neglected to mention him. The truth is I am not a great fan
of Liebling — no reason for you not to be. For me, he tries too hard to be
literary or artful. It's true that he was immensely talented. Like his pal
Mitchell, he started out as a newspaper reporter. Mitchell was the gentle,
shy southerner and the slowest of writers. Liebling was a brash, sassy New
Yorker and the fastest of writers. He wrote about nearly everything: Paris;
the French people; food; horse racing; the American press; Broadway
sharpers whom he called "Telephone-booth Indians"; and Chicago as the
"second city," its fault being that it wasn't New York. He did a book on the
"Earl" of Louisiana, Earl Long. Furthermore, as an eminent World War II
correspondent, Liebling accompanied the D-Day Normandy landings and
the allied forces' arrival into Paris where, "For the first time in my life I
have lived for a week in a great city where everybody was happy." The
French government gave Liebling the Legion d'Honneur for his wartime
reporting.

On the other hand — in addition to my aforementioned reservations about
his writing — it turns out that Liebling's most famous book is on boxing,
The Sweet Science. I am either too timid, or advanced, or puritanical, or
civilized, but I really don't approve of boxing. So you should "Check it out,"
as the youngsters say, and tell me what you think.

Irving

*

137

From: L.Dickerson@verizon.net
To: Irving.Gross@ns.edu
November 23, 2012

Dear Irving

You asked for it. I checked out The Sweet Science, and have read the whole damn thing cover to cover in a day and a half. It appeared first as articles for The New Yorker about the boxing world of the early 1950s. Back then, boxing was a big deal: Joe Louis, Jersey Joe Walcott, Rocky Marciano, and Archie Moore were national figures. I can see what you mean by "literary" – with references to Herodotus, Froissart, Rowlandson (who they?), and even Dickens.

The final chapter of the book culminates in the Marciano/Moore fight of September 15, 1955. Slugger vs artistic boxer. Here are some brief excerpts, my timid Irving: Nothing much happens in the first round, but the second round prompts Liebling to say that Moby Dick would be "just another fish story" if Ahab had succeeded. He recounts how Moore in this round hit Marciano squarely "with classic gravity and conciseness." But Marciano jumped up after two seconds, and Moore may have felt "like Don Giovanni when the Commendatore's statue grabbed at him – startled because he thought he had killed the guy already – or like Ahab when he saw the whale take down Fedallah, harpoons and all."

In the third round, Marciano waded in, "hurling his fists with a sublime disregard of probabilities, content to hit an elbow, a biceps, a shoulder, the top of the head....The crowd, basically anti-intellectual, screamed encouragement. There was Moore, riding punches, picking them off, slipping them, rolling with them, ducking them, coming gracefully out of his defensive efforts with sharp, patterned blows."

But by the fourth round, "Sisyphus began to get the idea that he couldn't roll back the rock." In the sixth Marciano knocked Moore down twice.

Then, in the seventh, "the embattled intellect put up its finest stand. Marciano powered out of his corner to finish Moore, and the stylist made him miss so often that it looked, for a fleeting moment, as if the champion were indeed punching himself arm-weak....In the eighth, the champion overflowed Archie. He knocked him down six seconds before the bell, and I don't think he could have got up by ten. Moore came out proudly for the ninth, and stood and fought back with all he had, but Marciano slugged him down and he was counted out.... It was a bruising defeat for the higher faculties and a lesson in intellectual humility, but Moore had made it a hell of a fight."

Sorry for all the quotations, but I know you won't read the book. By me, it's pretty terrific. This is not the kind of sports writing you see in the <u>Daily News</u> or for that matter in the <u>New York Times</u>. Much as fight fans regret that Liebling didn't live to report on the Ali-Frazer battles, and the fact that he covered boxing only from 1951 to 1955, still, as late as 2002, <u>Sports Illustrated</u> named <u>The Sweet Science</u> the "number one sports book of all time."

I immediately used Netflix to order the number one boxing movie of all time, "Raging Bull," of course. How DeNiro gained, and later lost, that weight is beyond me.

You know I love to run on in emails.

Larry

Liebling begins one of his long pieces dissecting American press coverage of Stalin's death with these words: "Inconsiderate to the last, Josef Stalin, a man who never had to meet a deadline, had the bad taste to die in installments."

✱

From: Irving.Gross@ns.edu
To: L.Dickerson@verizon.net
November 23, 2012

Dear Larry

Very impressive, your lengthy excerpts from <u>The Sweet Science</u>. With me, it's not just boxing I don't care for; I'm not a sports fan generally, not even of harmless sports like baseball. I know you are a sports fan, and your letter certainly reflects it. As for DeNiro, I have read that he gained the weight by eating at expensive restaurants in Paris. There must be worse ways to gain weight.

Irving

*

From: L.Dickerson@verizon.net
To: Irving.Gross@ns.edu
November 24, 2012

Dear Irving

    Liebling's first editions are only $200-$300. I'll get Between Meals: An Appetite for Paris – a gift for Melanie who loves cooking, food, and Paris. Of course there are a million books on cooking, so no one is going to vote Liebling the best in that category. Although, I'd bet he is very good on food. His attitude towards food was "not only qualitative but quantitative" – he insisted on enormous portions, what he called "eating with ambition." He became rotund. He probably ate himself to death.

Larry

Liebling once said that freedom of the press is only for those who own one.
    Total outlay to date: $28,300.

*

140

From: L.Dickerson@verizon.net
To: Irving.Gross@ns.edu
November 25, 2012

Dear Irving

    A quick follow-up. I know you are not a great fan of A.J. Liebling, and I won't try to convert you, but at the Strand I picked up a biography of Liebling called <u>Wayward Reporter</u> by Raymond Sokolov. I said earlier that Liebling "probably ate himself to death." No "probably" about it, according to Sokolov, who carefully documents Liebling's fatal eating habits. He was a hedonistic gourmand. A typical "lunch" would include two double martinis, two dozen oysters, two double portions of lobster fra diablo followed by osso buco with bottles of wine to match.

Larry

Liebling could not stand to put live lobsters in boiling water, so he first "drowned" them in a gallon of white wine at room temperature until they were supposedly so drunk they would not feel the pain.

*

From: Irving.Gross@ns.edu
To: L.Dickerson@verizon.net
November 26, 2012

Larry, the lobster business almost raises my sympathy for this apostle of boxing.

Irving

CHAPTER FIFTEEN

From: L.Dickerson@verizon.net
To: Charlie.Dover@duquest.co.uk
November 26, 2012

Dear Charlie

Just a line to say my collecting is coming along nicely, Thurber, Joseph Mitchell, and even Nabokov and Salinger.

I send you also a related bit of book news: I bumped into a woman, Susan Barile, who used to come into the bank years ago. And it turns out that she managed the famous Gotham Book Mart on 47th Street for years. There it was, one really good bookstore, among all the goddam diamond and jewelry dealers. Well, of course the Gotham Book Mart is long gone. (At least the Gotham Bar and Grill is still operating down here in the Village. I was there once with my wife, a hundred years ago, for a big anniversary. It's very expensive, of course. But one of the best and most famous restaurants in the city.) I started to tell Susan about the MacDowell letters. "Really," she said, "is that you, the editor? I know that book. I'm working on Victorian novelists." Well, Christ, you can imagine how thrilled I was to hear that. So we sat down for a coffee and exchanged stories. She is still "marginally" in the book business — told me she had 10 or 12 thousand books in a barn in upstate New York. But she has switched to going back to school and is nearing her PhD in English. Studying the Victorians. Then I told her I would email her with a few book questions from time to time if she didn't mind, and I added that after I have made some real progress with my collection I'll have her and her husband (he teaches at CUNY Lehman) over to look at my "Collection." That word still seems too grand for me. She said they'd love that. Nice person.

So now I have another book friend. I think too that I should contact that young woman (named Julia Rodas) who helped me edit my great great grandfather's letters.

Larry

Can you believe I'm collecting J.D. Salinger? Total outlay is $28,300 – not bad considering I spent almost $24,000 on the Victorians. But bad enough.

*

From: Charlie.Dover@duquest.co.uk
To: L.Dickerson@verizon.net
27 November 2012

Dear Larry

That's good that you have another book friend. The book world is a somewhat rarified place, and the more people you know in it the more knowledgeable a collector you will become.

Charlie

Salinger is indeed a "hot" author in the sense of being much sought after by collectors. The truth is I have never been a Salinger fan. Maybe you need to be an American to appreciate his genius.

* * *

From: L.Dickerson@verizon.net
To: SusanBarile1@yahoo.com
November 28, 2012

Dear Susan

Really good to meet up with you the other day. Already I'm about to start feeding you questions – since you said that was OK. Can you give me the names of used and rare book stores that just might have books by early New Yorker writers? I already know about:

143

The Strand (of course)
The Argosy
James Cummins
Bauman
Manhattan Rare Books
Osgood

   I know that Sotheby's and of course Christie's here in New York have auctions on books every once in a while – though I think these places are way out of my price range. Any other suggestions?

                                          Larry

                            *

From: SusanBarile1@yahoo.com
To: L.Dickerson@verizon.net
November 28, 2012

Hi Larry

Yes, it was nice to meet up with you. I look forward to your someday having John and me over to look at the results of your collecting.

As for old, used, and rare books, since you're now looking for 20th century books, you can pretty much go into any used book store and ask about the <u>New Yorker</u> writers you mentioned. (You're not looking for 17th century books.) There's also Westside Books, and Ursus, where a friend of mine works. And do try Left Bank Books, right here in the far West Village. He deals in "modern firsts" and has very reasonable prices.

And you can go online to most of these places. Also, it doesn't cost anything to look, even at Sotheby's or Christie's. Swann Auction Galleries is a little less pricy.

Yours
Susan

Do you read mysteries? Do you know John Dunning's books? He has a series of five or six murder mysteries about a cop in Denver turned used-book seller named Cliff Janeway. These books are really quick reading and there is a good deal of booklore tucked away in them. You can get them, and practically any crime mystery, at the "Partners and Crime" mystery bookshop on Greenwich Avenue, not far from your place.

*

From: L.Dickerson@verizon.net
To: SusanBarile1@yahoo.com
December 1, 2012

Dear Susan

Christ, I hardly know you and you had me up till the wee hours last night. I started reading John Dunning's <u>Booked to Die</u> and just would not quit. I myself don't like cliches like "page turner" and "couldn't put it down" – me having become a sort of a snob in regard to cliches. But only when I recognize them.
But I loved this book. Couldn't put it down.
Are all mysteries good like this? Probably not.

Larry

I see that Partners and Crime is about to close. Discouraging.

*

From: SusanBarile1@yahoo.com
To: L.Dickerson@verizon.net
December 2, 2012

Hi Larry

Yes, sad about Partners and Crime.

No, all mysteries aren't as good as that one, but Dunning's books are pretty even. You might read another one or two. Of course not all mystery readers like Dunning and plenty of other readers dislike all mysteries. Edmund Wilson, the famous man of letters and critic, hated the very idea of a detective mystery, and when friends prevailed on him to read a classic mystery by Dorothy Sayers, <u>Nine Tailors</u>, he called it, in <u>The New Yorker</u>, "one of the dullest books I have ever read." He called mysteries a "sub-literary genre."

No arguing about tastes, right? And there are plenty of mediocre and bad mysteries. Someone once said that there are as many mediocre straight novels as there are mediocre crime novels, the difference being that the latter get published. Then too, many famous people were devoted to reading mysteries, FDR, JFK, Clinton; and many writers including Updike and even Thurber, whom you have started collecting. In addition, I find that Gordon Ray, who in his day was the foremost Victorianist in the world, and whom friends of mine had in class at NYU back in the 70s and 80s, devoured fifty or so mysteries a year.

Do you know the books about book collecting by Nancy and Lawrence Goldstone? Especially the one called <u>Warmly Inscribed</u>?

Susan

*

From: L.Dickerson@verizon.net
To: SusanBarile1@yahoo.com
December 3, 2012

Dear Susan,

Actually, I have read Warmly Inscribed. The long chapter on the New England Forger and all that business about forged inscriptions and signatures really put the fear of God into me. Well, not the fear of God, not for me, but it has me a little worried. I have been buying various inscribed books, especially from a high-end dealer, Phillip Osgood.

I learned a few things from that chapter, chiefly that if you see a book signed or inscribed offered at a price way below what it should be, if it seems too good to be true, then it probably is too good to be true.

Evidently, in addition to faked signatures and inscriptions, there are various other shenanigans going on in the book world: for example, dust jackets "professionally restored" and the careful removal of the front end paper (where owners often put their signatures) because a signature there, unless by a famous person, cuts greatly into the value of a book – it's "defacing" it. I myself have defaced a few copies of The MacDowell Correspondence.

Mysteries – you certainly have converted me with that John Dunning book. The name Gordon Ray rings a bell with me, because I bought his two-volume biography of my favorite novelist – or I should say of the author of my all-time favorite novel, Vanity Fair. By now I have read a second Dunning mystery, The Bookman's Wake. As you told me, you can pick up quite a bit of information on book collecting in Dunning's books. He has plenty about the difference between "scarce" and "rare" books, and about "points" – like "a battered d on p 220." Also on the evil of putting "embosser marks" on books, "like branding cattle – to show possession," and the "defiling" of remaindered books with a black line across the closed top pages.

Dunning has Cliff Janeway say, "You need a bookman's eye to appreciate what a perfect copy of a fifty-year old book looks like. It does not look like a new book – it looks so wonderfully like an old book that's never been touched." Dunning also has some good stuff on the thrill of being in the hunt, etc, and on how for some people looking at books is like making love. I don't know about that.

   And finally there's the line, "A (new) book has always cost about what a meal in a good restaurant costs." I suppose a paperback should cost what a good cheeseburger costs.

Larry

PS But I see Dunning has his main character Janeway say something about "the enormity of the book business," Booked To Die, page 198. Maybe I'll give up on the word "enormity."

CHAPTER SIXTEEN

From: L.Dickerson@verizon.net
To: SusanBarile1@yahoo.com
December 5, 2012

Dear Susan

I just got back from the Left Bank Book Shop in the West Village. I should have gone there much earlier. I love the place. It is a picture-perfect version of the small Greenwich Village book shop. And they have great books in the window, with identifying cards as to edition and date – not prices. They had, for example, Gabriel Garcia Marquez's first English edition of One Hundred Years of Solitude; and Tennessee William's The Glass Menagerie. While I was there a young woman came into the store all excited about having seen that first edition of The Glass Menagerie in the window – until she was told it was $750. She said she would think about it and come back when she could afford it. (She was probably an aspiring actress.) But, what really caught my eye in the window was an original Lolita, the Paris edition, boxed.

I managed to strike up a conversation with the owner, Kim Herzinger. We talked about book prices and book-selling. He handles chiefly 20th century books, "modern firsts." He also told me that virtually all rare book dealers keep up a connection with Abebooks. He talked about the inflation of the traditional "grades" given books, especially on the internet. "Poor," "Fair," "Good," "Very Good," "Near Fine," and "Fine." Fine means pretty much free of any defects. Near Fine is a kind of A-. The problem is that sellers, knowing that collectors don't want anything beat up, often advertise books as "Very Good" that are really not good at all. The description "Fair" usually means a wreck. He said Abebooks takes 12 to 15% on sales. Makes you wonder what those small dealer guys are making who sell books on Abebooks for $1.00. He himself advertises on Abebooks but only does about 10% of his business on internet sales.

He had some books that are on my list. I bought a beautiful copy of A.J. Liebling's <u>The Earl of Louisiana</u>. And one of Joe Mitchell's, <u>Old Mr. Flood</u> (At $200 and $300). Thanks for steering me to Left Bank Books.

Larry

* * *

From: L.Dickerson@verizon.net
To: Irving.Gross@ns.edu
December 7, 2012

Dear Irving

    I visited Left Bank Books in the West Village today for my second time in three days. It's the kind of store I'd love to be able to hang around in and shoot the book breeze. On my second visit I got gabbing (again) with the owner. Told him about the MacDowell letters. I told him I was grateful for all the book collecting information he had given me on my first visit to the shop. After putzing around a bit, I asked Kim if I could see the <u>Lolita</u>, the first edition, boxed, Paris, 2 volumes. He was kind enough to take this precious item out of the window to show me. He opened the box and took out the two slim and fragile paperbound volumes. Cost: $4,000. This copy is not, he admits, in the very best condition. He has it on consignment at that price, but if it were in "fine" condition, it would be $10,000.
    I told him how a year or so ago a friend of mine (you) had insisted that I read <u>One Hundred Years of Solitude</u>. Kim then told me that the English edition, besides being extraordinarily high priced, has only one "point" that constitutes the difference between a true first printing and the second and later printings. Namely, that there is an exclamation point that was removed from the inside front jacket text after the first printing. His copy has the exclamation mark. That exclamation mark might be worth a thousand dollars.
    I then told him that I have a friend – you again – who met Marquez's

150

translator, Gregory Rabassa, and asked him about Marquez never using -mente ("-ly") adverbs. Kim said he didn't remember hearing about Marquez's never using "-ly" adverbs, but that he was interested to learn about it. Book people like little anecdotes like that, don't they? They don't deal with big things – like politics or war – so they talk about things like this "-ly" business or "points" like that exclamation mark.

He told me how naive book buyers come in and ask if he has any Jane Austen: "Do you have any first editions of Pride and Prejudice or Emma?" He tells them "No, I don't have first editions of those books, and I don't think you would want to spend the many thousands of dollars they would cost you if I did."

Larry

Total outlay to date: $28,800.

✳ ✳ ✳

From: L.Dickerson@verizon.net
To: Kimherzinger@gmail.com
December 12, 2012

Dear Kim

Just a line to say how much I enjoyed meeting you and seeing your shop – and making some good purchases.

Larry

✳

From: Kimherzinger@gmail.com
To: L.Dickerson@verizon.net
December 12, 2012

Dear Larry

I also much enjoyed our talks. It's good to find a really enthusiastic
collector here in the Village. Well, I am not "here" now but down in Texas
where I teach English Literature at the University of Houston-Victoria. My
very capable assistants run the shop most of the time. I must thank you,
again, for the copy of <u>The MacDowell Correspondence</u>. What a
wonderful thing that was for you to have inherited letters to your great
great grandfather from the likes of Dickens, Thackeray, Trollope, George
Eliot, Hardy and others. You have edited them nicely. I particularly like the
Thackeray letters. What a stylist he was, dashing off wondrous sentences
in quickly composed letters – the equivalent of a phone call or an email
today. Let's keep in touch.

Kim

*

From: L.Dickerson@verizon.net
To: Kimherzinger@gmail.com
December 13, 2012

Dear Kim

    Thanks for the note. I probably enjoyed our talks more than you did,
but we won't argue it. To think that your wonderful West Village shop
has been there all along and I didn't realize it.
    Yes, let's keep in touch. I was in the shop the other day and they told
me you would be back around spring break and early June.

                                                              Larry

From: L.Dickerson@verizon.net
To: Nicholls@btinternet.com
December 14, 2012

Dear Stephen,

No emergency, just thought to say hello and tell you I have collected many of the Victorian novels mentioned in the MacDowell letters and have passed on to early New Yorker writers. My friend Irving Gross is guiding me through writers like Thurber, Salinger, Mitchell, Liebling, Nabokov, et al. So I pass on to you a very short short story you might think funny.

Among New Yorker writers I discovered John McNulty, who died in 1956. My favorite is very short, from 1941, called "Atheist Hit by Truck": A drunk was walking in the street near 42nd Street and Third Avenue, and a truck knocks him down. A crowd gathers. Then a young cop arrives and sits him up on a stoop. The drunk is not hurt too bad, but an ambulance from Bellevue is called. The cop takes down his name and address and then asks him his religion. The drunk says, "Atheist, I'm an atheist." Some in the crowd laugh, and a hack driver says, "Jeez, he's an atheist!" An older cop arrives and tells the young cop that he is to rub out "atheist" in the report and put in "Cat'lic." – "He looks like a Cat'lic to me." The drunk protests he's an atheist. The older cop tells him, "If you wouldn't go around saying you're an atheist, maybe you wouldn't be gettin' hit by trucks." The crowd senses "a great moral lesson." The hackie says again, "Jeez! the guy says he is an atheist." The drunk keeps muttering "I yama natheist" as they put him into the ambulance to Bellevue.

This McNulty is the guy who for a while deserted Harold Ross and The New Yorker to go to Hollywood and write for Paramount Pictures. Ross was incensed at his leaving, but closed by saying, "Well, God bless you, McNulty, goddam it."

You too, Stephen.

Larry

153

*

From: Nicholls@btinternet.com
To: L.Dickerson@verizon.net
15 December 2012

Dear Larry

Thanks. Good to hear from you. Glad to learn your project is coming along nicely. Your recent focus, though pretty wide, sounds good. You could do worse than Thurber, Updike, Salinger, and Nabokov.

Stephen

PS You could have just sent me the title: "Atheist Hit by Truck" does it for me all by itself.

*   *   *

From: L.Dickerson@verizon.net
To: Irving.Gross@ns.edu
December 15, 2012

Dear Irving

    You never mentioned John McNulty to me. For six dollars at the Strand I picked up This Place on Third Avenue, a little book put together by his widow in 2001. If I am to believe the puffs on the cover, McNulty was an important New Yorker writer, mentioned in the same breath with Joseph Mitchell and Damon Runyon. I get a kick out of the saloon stories. He writes in the tone of his characters. Everyone says he had a "good ear." He wrote more than 60 stories for The New Yorker.

Larry

154

*

From: Irving.Gross@ns.edu
To: L.Dickerson@verizon.net
December 16, 2012

Dear Larry

Yes, I was going to mention McNulty. (There are plenty more New Yorker writers. I figured you should start slowly.) McNulty's books should not cost you too much: A Man Gets Around, Third Avenue, New York, and My Son Johnny.

I myself own a collection called The World of John McNulty, with a glowing introduction by Thurber, saying that McNulty was the funniest man he ever knew, and a "raconteur rampant." According to Thurber, McNulty as a young newspaperman almost singlehandedly "ridiculed the Ku Klux Klan out of existence" in Columbus, Ohio, in the 1920s. McNulty saw the world in his own special way; his imagination was always cooking. He would say things like, "1885 was the year the owls were so bad"; or that "Girls named Dolores become hairdressers"; that "All watch repairers are named Schneider." He had perfect pitch for Third Avenue saloon parlance, and without the slightest condescension produced the everyday speech of ordinary people: The bartender who said, "He's Irish and he broods easy"; "The lady was a Bostonian, they call them."

Whenever McNulty liked a book, he couldn't wait to give it away to some friend.

H. L. Mencken, another New Yorker writer who admired McNulty's stuff, said, "This is writing. This is it."

Irving

*

155

From: L.Dickerson@verizon.net
To: Irving.Gross@ns.edu
December 16, 2012

Dear Irving

On the basis of This Place on Third Avenue, I'll be chasing down McNulty's New Yorker books. I gather from the internet that his books are inexpensive. Time has not been as kind to McNulty as it has been to Mitchell and even Liebling. Back at Left Bank Books I got an inscribed Third Avenue for $125; and A Man Gets Around, inscribed, "For Daise Terry, without whom there would be no New Yorker writers' books, John McNulty." That's nice, isn't it? – giving the office secretary credit. This copy is only $150. My pile of inscribed copies grows steadily. My Son Johnny was too sentimental for The New Yorker (I can hear Ross saying, "This isn't the goddamned Saturday Evening Post"). It was published in Woman's Day. A first edition is very cheap today – about $100.

Of course I got talking there at Left Bank Books with Kim Herzinger. I told him how I had swapped in my early copies of Vanity Fair and Orley Farm for signed copies. He wanted to know where I got them, and I said Phillip Osgood. It turns out that Osgood bought some books from him (dealers, as you most likely know, get an automatic 20% discount from other dealers). Herzinger said, "God knows what he charges his clients uptown for these downtown purchases. Two or three times what he pays me." I said something like "He's always very cordial with me." And Herzinger says, "Oh, he's 'cordial' all right. A very smooth-talking, high-end dealer." I didn't know exactly what he meant by this, and I didn't know him well enough to ask. So I just said that I always feel a little awkward around Osgood, and Herzinger said, "Yeah, I know what you mean. I think he's a bit full of himself. He certainly is sure of himself. Just be careful." I said something like I know I have to be cautious in dealing with him as he certainly is a convincing salesman.

The conversation moved on, and he asked me to guess which Victorian book most people asked for in his store – he gave me two guesses – I wanted to say Vanity Fair but I knew that was dead wrong. So I guessed Copperfield or Tess of the D'Urbervilles. Then in the same breath I snuck in two more – Wuthering Heights or Jane Eyre. He said those were all good guesses, but no, it was Alice in Wonderland. What can you say? When I got home, I found out on the internet that Lewis Carroll, or rather I should use his real name, Charles Dodgson, disliked the very first printing of Alice, and he had the print-run of 2,000 copies withdrawn. All but a handful of early copies were retrieved. Then Dodgson and his publisher – Macmillan – sold the remaining 1,900 plus sets of sheets to Appleton's in New York, who had them bound (in England) with their own title page, which in 1866 became the first "obtainable" edition. A "very good copy" of this American edition – "some minor wear, dampstain and spots to cover" – costs you $23,000. As for the original withdrawn 1865 English edition, only about 20 or so are known to have survived. One is in Madrid, of all places, and is for sale for $170,000 – with condition described as "pobre"!

Larry

Total outlay to date: $29,425. The fiscal year is over; that total puts me $4,425 past my original $25,000 but $575 within my "revised" $30,000.

CHAPTER SEVENTEEN

From: L.Dickerson@verizon.net
To: Irving.Gross@ns.edu
December 17, 2012

Dear Irving

Like I once or twice told you, I would just love to see what the New Yorker offices look like today compared to how they were in the old days as described by writers like Thurber and Brendan Gill. So today I called the New Yorker offices, explaining my collecting project and saying I would appreciate having a "most brief look around the place." A snippy young woman in the publicity department told me to put my request to her in an email. I did so, mentioning how I was collecting first editions of New Yorker writers, although only God knows if she ever even heard of most of the ones I listed. And of course I told her how my MacDowell Correspondence got a "briefly noted" review in the magazine. Then this same woman answers me by email saying that they get "countless requests of this kind all the time, and unfortunately have to decline them all." Christ, I don't believe that they get requests every day from someone as serious as I am about the magazine, not to mention my book having been reviewed there – though only on the "Briefly Noted" page.

Fircrissakes, I was only asking for ten minutes.

Larry

*

From: Irving.Gross@ns.edu
To: L.Dickerson@verizon.net
December 17, 2012

Dear Larry

I can see that this is a sore point with you, and I don't blame you, what
with your book being reviewed, however briefly, in the magazine. I have a
friend at Harvard, Louis Menand, who writes regularly for the magazine,
and I will email him your request for a "quick look around" the New
Yorker offices.

Your wanting to see the place is part of the "hero worship" that many
readers and collectors share with you: Dickens lovers who want to see
the Dickens House on Doughty Street in London; or people here in New
York who go to the White Horse Tavern in the West Village to see where
Dylan Thomas drank himself to death. I don't share that kind of
enthusiasm, as you know. But I think I understand it.

Irving

*

From: Irving.Gross@ns.edu
To: L.Dickerson@verizon.net
December 18, 2012

Dear Larry

Thanks to Luke Menand, you have an appointment with a New Yorker
editor named Nigel Hanley, for a "quick look around" on Thursday at 3 pm.

Irving

From: L.Dickerson@verizon.net
To: Irving.Gross@ns.edu
December 18, 2012

Dear Irving

   Christ, that is wonderful. Thank you. I know of course that the offices
are <u>entirely</u> different from the times in the old building with my heroes,
Ross, Thurber, Salinger, and Nabokov. Still, this collector would like to see
the present place. Call it hero-worship or misguided enthusiasm or
whatever, but that's me.
   Again, a thousand thanks. A regular goddam Christmas present!

                                        Your relic-kissing friend
                                        Larry

                          *

From: L.Dickerson@verizon.net
To: Irving.Gross@ns.edu
December 21, 2012

Dear Irving

   What a wonderful visit I had at the <u>New Yorker</u> offices. I simply must
tell you all about the place. And this Nigel Hanley, a very nice guy – he
sounded English to me – showed me around for more than half an hour.
Never mind ten minutes. But let me begin with the Conde Nast building
itself, a "towering skyscraper," even there among the many skyscrapers of
Midtown. Its address is "Four Times Square," and the building runs
through the entire block, so you can enter it either from 42nd Street or
43rd Street. All glass and steel, of course. To get past the front desk you
have to prove you have an appointment at one of their magazines, <u>Vogue</u>,
<u>Glamour</u>, <u>Wired</u>, <u>GQ</u>, <u>Golf Today</u>, etc. I showed them the email from
Nigel Hanley, and the security fellow behind the desk told me I was "eight
minutes early." I nearly said, "Well, pardon me for committing such an

outrage." Instead, I meekly agreed I was eight minutes early. But, shortly, this security person relented and called upstairs, asked for a photo ID, and gave me a visitor's pass (I still have it, a souvenir!). On the 20th floor Nigel Hanley met me in the New Yorker lobby. I was in!

Nigel Hanley was most friendly. By way of introduction I had not only your Louis Menand connection, but it seems that Hanley's girlfriend, a PhD candidate, took a Victorian novel seminar that you gave up at the CUNY Graduate School, and – get this – she has actually read the MacDowell Correspondence! Just a few degrees of separation, as they say. Anyway, as you walk in from the lobby you are greeted by three "murals" that Thurber drew on the walls of the old place on 43rd Street. And next to these old yellowed pieces of plaster are framed originals by Thurber, Charles Addams, and Saul Steinberg. Can you guess what the Thurber cartoon was? "The Seal in the Bedroom." But all the inside walls are covered with pictures, photographs, and covers. In fact, on a couple of walls they tacked up all the New Yorker covers (one tack for each corner) from 1993 to the present. I was tempted to say that I have all of the last three years' covers, and if they ever noticed one missing – but I didn't.

As you walk around – you are practically walking around an entire city block – you come to many open offices with people working in cubicles. We walked past the fact checkers – about 15 or 16 of them (fact checkers, I was told, typically make inquiries such as, "Is it correct that so-and-so, born in 1945, was fifty-eight when he died in July 2003? What was his exact birthdate?"). About the same number of persons occupy another 15 cubicles doing copyediting, which here is called "Ok-ing" (Okers go into things like "than I" vs "than me," or "further" vs "farther"). There was another large open work area for web workers, plus separate rooms for various "libraries" – one for reference works for the fact checkers, and another for books by New Yorker writers. I should have liked to ask to see that one but I didn't want to use up my time. Another book room contained books recently received, candidates for review. Entire shelves are labeled, for example, "April fiction." The chances of getting reviewed are really slim – they get about 100 books a day before being winnowed down to those in the book room. Nigel admitted that the process of choosing to review a particular book was rather hit or miss – some editor or writer takes a fancy to a particular book, and it gets reviewed. They make no effort at wide book coverage. As you know, each issue has usually one long book review and four "briefly noted." That's five out of 700. You do the odds. How the MacDowell letters got that "Briefly Noted" review is beyond me. I don't know who wrote it because the briefly noted reviews are not signed.

He showed me the editor's office. David Remnick was not in, so we looked in from the door. It's a spectacular corner office with windows on the two outside walls running pretty much floor to ceiling. Beautiful. I saw a large and striking photograph of John Updike. I asked about staff writers like Adam Gopnik — he has his own office of course, but he was away for the day and his door was closed. All told there are about 100 employees on the 20th (editorial) floor and maybe 50 on the business side, one floor up. He said that, like in the old days, there is strict "separation of church and state." And yes, he knew the ancient anecdote about someone from the business department of the old New Yorker offices getting off the elevator at the editorial floor, coming out with his hands up and saying, "Don't shoot, I have permission." I asked Nigel how a weekly magazine could support 150 employees, and he said that The New Yorker has "the highest subscription renewal rate of any magazine in the country." He said that somebody in, say, Texas, by subscribing to The New Yorker can think of himself as a bit aside from the ordinary human herd down there. And he faithfully renews. To my question about Conde Nast, he said they didn't interfere in the running of The New Yorker. Thank God for that, I thought.

Nigel explained how a manuscript, once accepted, goes first to an editor — there are a dozen or so senior editors and half a dozen assistant editors, of which Nigel Hanley is one. He said that some regular contributors, like Luke Menand, submit such finished manuscripts that they quickly flow through the system — editors, okers, and fact checkers. On the other hand, some other writers' manuscripts — he didn't volunteer any names — require a good deal of "tinkering" at the editor's level. I told Nigel that you lived in the same building for years with Joe Mitchell, and remarked how saddened everyone was that he had not left anything publishable behind. Nigel nodded, "But," he said, "we are hoping there may be material from the Salinger estate." He also mentioned a new biography coming out soon and a documentary and American Masters TV program on Salinger.

After we said goodbye, I sat down in one of the easy chairs in the lobby of the magazine, to gather my thoughts and to look around the room. It's decorated by about 20 large blow ups (each about four foot high) of New Yorker covers. They start at the beginning where you find the newsstand price was 15 cents in 1925, a price that stayed the same until the late 1940s. By 1974 it was 50 cents; in 1982 it was $1.50, and in 1998 it was $3.00. Today, as you know, the cover price is $6.99. An odd indicator of inflation? That is, the price today is about 47 times what it was in 1925 – with all the inflation coming after more than 20 years of that steady original price of 15 cents. (Actually that is not out of line; I find that the New York City subway fare stayed at a nickel until 1948 when it went to a dime. Today, as you well know it's $2.50, which is 50 times what it was in 1925.)

A young woman – obviously a staff employee – was hurrying into the office area and seeing me asked if she could be of any help. I said no thanks and explained how I had just met with Nigel Hanley and was looking at the cover reproductions on my way out. But I couldn't keep out of my mind Brendan Gill's account of the lack of sociability in the old days, how a new staff member had come upon an older colleague at the water cooler and said something like "I hope you had a pleasant weekend," and was answered, "Fuck you." Things change.

                                        Thanks again
                                        Larry

                            *

From: Irving.Gross@ns.edu
To: L.Dickerson@verizon.net
December 21, 2012

Dear Larry

Thanks for your report. I knew it would be lengthy and (you'll forgive me) "gushing." From the standpoint of someone like myself, who really doesn't give a damn about the building or the offices but who looks only to the contents, the texts (and pictures) themselves, I thought to myself how amazing it was that Harold Ross's "little comic magazine" has grown into the large and influential national institution that it is today, powered, as you say, by about 150 employees. But it's equally amazing that the magazine has maintained its identity, so much so that even now it seems closely to replicate the magazine founded by Ross in 1925 and which he, that eccentric genius, closely guided for the next quarter of a century. He's dead more than sixty years, and yet (aside from the "bedroom stuff" and some explicit language) he would, I think, recognize the magazine as his. Mutatis mutandis, as we say. But some things don't change.

Irving

*

From: L.Dickerson@verizon.net
To: Irving.Gross@ns.edu
December 22, 2012

Irving

  Now who's "gushing"? Mutatis mutandis yourself.

Larry

*

From: Irving.Gross@ns.edu
To: L.Dickerson@verizon.net
December 22, 2012

Dear Larry

I presume you have come down from the high of getting in to see the New Yorker offices.

As for myself, I've been reading an essay on book collectors by Walter Benjamin. Benjamin was a German Jew, a philosopher, intellectual, Marxist, literary and social critic, and first-rate (but difficult) writer. In 1940 he was fleeing the Nazis, escaped into Spain, but was told by the Spanish police that the next day he would be shipped back to Nazi-held France for all but certain execution. Believing this, he committed suicide.

Now I know philosophy doesn't really interest you, and I suspect you would find most of Benjamin "tough sledding," as you say, and not at all in your line of interest. But his 9-page paper (1931) on himself as a book collector made me think – mutatis mutandis again – of you, and even of myself. Benjamin doesn't highlight first editions – he simply collects all important books connected with his wide-ranging interests. Benjamin narrates how he has been travelling for two years and is now unpacking crates of his old books. His mood, he says, is not one of nostalgia, but one of "anticipation" because in speaking of his books he is really speaking of himself.

Benjamin defends private, personal libraries, like yours, like mine, like Spencer's. But for Benjamin private ownership leads the collector into a responsibility for his property. He writes that public collections "may be less objectionable socially, and more useful academically than private collections, but the objects get their due only in the latter."

Benjamin goes so far as to assert that the ownership of books by a collector "is the most intimate relationship that one can have to objects. Not that they come alive in him, but it is he who lives in them." Pretty high-flying claims. But remember Updike on Salinger, saying that the "willingness to risk excess [here Benjamin's claims] on behalf of one's obsessions is what distinguishes artists from entertainers." Collectors of other objects, like paintings, would also object to Benjamin's "most intimate" claim for book collectors – but there you have it.

Benjamin ends on a light note with the heresy: "O Bliss of the collector, bliss of the man of leisure! Of no one has less been expected, and no one has had a greater sense of well-being than the man who has been able to carry on his disreputable existence in the mask of Spitzweg's 'Bookworm.'"*

Irving

*German painter Carl Spitzweg's 1850 painting "The Bookworm" is meant to be satiric but seems also a loving rendition of an eccentric old bookman.

I attach the nine pages, and a scan. Not a very clear one, but you get the idea.

*

From: L.Dickerson@verizon.net
To: Irving.Gross@ns.edu
December 23, 2012

Dear Irving

    Thanks for the Walter Benjamin article. I will soon be able to say, for instance, "You know that Walter Benjamin said that a collector's relationship to his books is 'the most intimate' relationship that anyone can have to objects."

Larry

It will be a long time before I need a ladder to get to my books, which all together, paperbacks included, number about a hundred now. Merry Jewish Christmas.

CHAPTER EIGHTEEN

From: L.Dickerson@verizon.net
To: Julia.Rodas@yahoo.com
December 28, 2012

Dear Julia

How are you?

Sorry to bother you at the holiday season – Merry Christmas – but I have been thinking of you lately. It's been a few years since I hired you to help edit and prepare my MacDowell letters for publication. You were really a terrific help. As you know the MacDowell book got a tiny paragraph in The New Yorker. Of course getting into The New York Times is next to impossible, especially if your book is from a small publishing house.

But tell me how you are doing.

Can you believe I've started collecting rare books?

Larry

*

From: Julia.Rodas@yahoo.com
To: L.Dickerson@verizon.net
December 29, 2012

Hello Larry

Good to hear from you. It was enjoyable working with you on those letters.

Myself, I am out of the publishing world altogether for a few years now and am teaching at Bronx Community College, CUNY. I'm doing well there.

Tell me how you are. And what's this about book collecting?

Julia

Happy New Year.

*

From: L.Dickerson@verizon.net
To: Julia.Rodas@yahoo.com
January 2, 2013

Dear Julia

   Happy New Year. Great to hear from you after three years or whatever it is. Nice to be back in touch. I knew you had to go and get back into teaching – what's a PhD in English literature doing at some goddam publishing house anyway? Anyhow, I am glad to hear the good news, and I imagine that you are knocking them dead up there in the Bronx.
   Yes, I've become a book collector, of sorts. On a fairly minor scale. I have narrowed myself to two focuses. I am pretty well done collecting the novels featured in the MacDowell letters – David Copperfield, The Mill on the Floss, Vanity Fair (of course), etc. And again of course, Trollope's Last Chronicle and Orley Farm. But now I have taken to collecting books by early New Yorker writers – from when the magazine started in 1925 to about 1960. I can't get Harold Ross, the editor and founder, out of my mind. Of course he didn't write books himself but he had a genius for spotting talent – James Thurber, E. B. White, Joseph Mitchell, A.J. Liebling, J.D. Salinger, Nabokov, et al.

Yours
Larry

169

*

From: Julia.Rodas@yahoo.com
To: L.Dickerson@verizon.net
January 3, 2013

Hello Larry

Good to know you are still involved in writers, books, etc. Among your New Yorker people, I hope you have Dorothy Parker on your list; she's one of my interests. She is chiefly remembered as a wit. Everybody in the world knows she said

>   Men seldom make passes
>   At girls who wear glasses.

But she did a lot more than make smart remarks. She was a notable short story writer, critic, and poet (some called her "the flapper poet"). She was a founding member of the Algonquin Round Table in 1923. She was famous for satire and sexual explicitness and also for her unabashed amours. She made a number of attempts at suicide, which your hero Ross said could be "bad for her health." She had bouts of drinking problems. She was famously a leftist and an anti-establishment figure (the FBI had a 1,000-page dossier on her). Parker wrote for Hollywood but was blacklisted by the House Un-American Activities Committee. She was a staunch supporter of civil rights, especially for black people; she left her estate to Martin Luther King, Jr., which on King's death passed to the NAACP.

As I said, she is most celebrated for her wise cracks and word play: "Brevity is the soul of lingerie"; "It serves me right for keeping all my eggs in one bastard"; "Take care of the luxuries and the necessities will take care of themselves." As for The New Yorker, Parker was in at the founding of the magazine in 1925, an original board member. In the early days her short stories, poetry, reportage, and her "Constant Reader" column of book reviews played a major role in keeping the magazine afloat. Once, when she had not been in the office for a few days, she ran into Ross who asked her where she had been lately, and she said, "Someone was using the pencil." She also said that if the office she shared at the magazine with Robert Benchley "were an inch smaller, it would amount to adultery." Her early stories satirize society people, pretentious intellectuals (male and female), heavy drinkers, married men, married women. She was way ahead of her time, as in her depiction of white people who "know some nice Negroes" as long as "they know their place."

Julia

∗　∗　∗

From:　L.Dickerson@verizon.net
To:　　Irving.Gross@ns.edu
January 4, 2013

Dear Irving,

　　The woman friend of mine who helped me edit the MacDowell letters says I must not forget Dorothy Parker.

Larry

∗

From:　Irving.Gross@ns.edu
To:　　L.Dickerson@verizon.net
January 5, 2013

Dear Larry

Of course Dorothy Parker – a fine writer but most remembered for her conversational wit. If I were asked to rattle off the great wits, I'd say:

171

Samuel Johnson, Sydney Smith, Oscar Wilde, Max Beerbohm, and
Dorothy Parker.

Mention of her brings to mind a remarkable trait in Ross, whom you find
so captivating: he was very prudish in regard to women and generally
uneasy in their company. He preferred the company of men, where he
could complain, "I'm surrounded by women and children." But his
biographer, Thomas Kunkel, writes that for all his Victorian attitudes
towards most women, he could appreciate and work with women of
talent: Katharine Angell (later Mrs White), Lois Long, Dorothy Parker,
Janet Flanner, and (illustrator) Helen Hokinson." Later Ross would
champion Lillian Ross (no relation!), Rebecca West ("best damned
reporter out there"), and Mary McCarthy.

And of course there was Shirley Jackson and her horror story "The
Lottery," which Ross published by overruling his editors. "The Lottery"
prompted hundreds of readers to cancel their subscriptions. Shirley
Jackson received a deluge of hate mail and even death threats. From this
distance the fracas tells us much about the country itself, especially
suburban America, in the post-war period. That Americans could have
been so violently upset by this fable about evil traditions lingering on into
the present is a story in itself. But, slowly, "The Lottery" became accepted
as one of the great short pieces in American fiction. It seems that every
high school or college student in the country has read it somewhere along
the line. In 1950 Farrar, Straus and Giroux jumped in immediately and
published a collection, The Lottery and Other Stories, but nobody really
wanted her other stories, and you don't hear much about the book today.

But Dorothy Parker, yes, by all means. And that one book by Shirley
Jackson.

Irving

*

From: L.Dickerson@verizon.net
To: Irving.Gross@ns.edu
January 7, 2013

Dear Irving

Fircrissakes, even I had to read "The Lottery" in high school. I just read it again after almost 50 years. Even though I knew the story and the ending, it <u>still</u> gave me the creeps. Christ, this is powerful stuff. Could anything be more horrible than those closing words about the villagers taking up stones – "and then they were upon her."

I'm laying out $100 for the first edition of the book. It would fit in nicely – while showing my <u>New Yorker</u> collection, I'll say, "Oh, and yes, here is the first appearance, between hard covers, of Shirley Jackson's story 'The Lottery.'"

And I'll certainly look into Dorothy Parker.

Larry

Total outlay to date: $29,535

*   *   *

From: L.Dickerson@verizon.net
To: Julia.Rodas@yahoo.com
January 10, 2013

Dear Julia

I've picked up a modern copy of Dorothy Parker's collected stories, <u>Laments for the Living</u>, which contains "The Big Blonde." That's her best-known story, or so the back cover says. I just finished reading "The Big Blonde." Christ, that story is depressing. I suppose when you know that Dorothy Parker herself had an alcohol problem and attempted suicide a number of times, you can see where this story is coming from. I am almost afraid to read the rest of them. Are they all downers like "Big Blonde"?

Larry

*

From: Julia.Rodas@yahoo.com
To: L.Dickerson@verizon.net
January 12, 2013

Hello Larry

Well, it's called Laments for the Living, isn't it? And "Big Blonde" was not a New Yorker story. In its early days The New Yorker printed only short short fiction. And "Big Blonde" is pretty long. Moreover, not all her stories are depressing or sad. I readily concede that she's not everyone's cup of tea. But you must read more. Get her Penguin Collected Stories.

Julia

*

From: L.Dickerson@verizon.net
To: Julia.Rodas@yahoo.com
January 14, 2013

Dear Julia

    Right. I tried a few more, once my nerve was back up. The back cover says the stories explore the "cruel superficialities of social behavior" and reveal "a deep sadness beneath the caustic wit." They sure do.

Larry

Despite my jitters, I've got a $300 copy of Laments for the Living with a

174

dust jacket. From Left Bank Books. The owner threw in gratis a modern edition of her New Yorker book reviews called Constant Reader.

*

From: L.Dickerson@verizon.net
To: Julia.Rodas@yahoo.com
January 14, 2013

Dear Julia

A quick follow up. I take it back. I've read quite a few other stories by Dorothy Parker (I've really come to generally like short stories). Thanks for bringing her to my attention. She's as satiric as hell about damn near everything, especially men of all stripes.

In good old Three Lives Book Store I spotted that Penguin Classic Complete Short Stories you mentioned to me – only $15 and what a beautifully funny cover by that Al Hirschfeld. There's genius for you. I'd love to own an original cartoon of his. I imagine his originals are very expensive.

Larry

*

From: L.Dickerson@verizon.net
To: Julia.Rodas@yahoo.com
January 15, 2013

Dear Julia

I've finished Dorothy Parker's complete short stories and read something about her in a biography. The joke is I think I have actually developed a kind of imaginary crush on this woman who has been dead almost fifty years. Or at least this is what my real life girlfriend Melanie

175

thinks (you met her once). She bases her scandalous claim on the way I talk about Dorothy Parker and her work. What a life she had – so brave and so tough and so talented. Blacklisted from Hollywood for a dozen years by those right-wing bastards.

Larry

*　*　*

From:　L.Dickerson@verizon.net
To:　　Charlie.Dover@duquest.co.uk
January 16, 2013

Dear Charlie,

Just reporting in. A very late Happy New Year to you.

I'm collecting Dorothy Parker. Melanie says I have a crush on her. Very funny.

Larry

Total outlay to date: $29,639.

This means I got through my first year slightly under my "revised" budget of $30,000. But that year was my big splurge start. It was also my year for expensive Victorian writers. Let's see if I can keep this next year to a mere $5,000, or so.

I send an Al Hirschfeld drawing of Dorothy Parker from the cover of the Penguin Classic of her collected stories.

*

From: Charlie.Dover@duquest.co.uk
To: L.Dickerson@verizon.net
17 January 2013

Dear Larry

It's not a joke if you'd rather stay home reading Parker's complete short stories when you should be out with Melanie seeing "To Rome with Love" or other movies.

Charlie

Thanks for the Hirschfeld. We of course have Penguin Classics in the UK, but I might never have seen that cover. A belated happy New Years to you, too. Yes, I suggest you go easy on the spending this year.

*

From: L.Dickerson@verizon.net
To: Charlie.Dover@duquest.co.uk
January 18, 2013

Dear Doctor Charlie

I'm still doing my best about getting out more. In fact we looked at "To Rome with Love." Not one of Allen's best. Mentioning Woody Allen reminds me that Melanie and Allen graduated from the same school, Midwood High School in Brooklyn. She was years later of course. Melanie was voted "the prettiest girl" in the graduating class (1,000 strong). She tells the story that she came home, and her father (he was a doctor) was going through his mail and she said, "Daddy, daddy, I was voted prettiest girl in the graduating class." He just kept going through his mail and without looking up said, "Who got the smartest?" She doesn't particularly like me retelling this story although I think it is really funny. But it's sad too. Some of my friends say it is a Jewish story. I don't know what makes a story a Jewish story. There are a lot of American Jewish comedians, beginning for me at least with Jack Benny – but also Alan King, Buddy Hackett, the Marx Brothers, Billy Crystal, Jackie Mason. Christ, all the American comics were Jewish!

Melanie and I had a little sit-down dinner party of my book friends. But my books were not the center of attention. The real hit was Melanie's osso buco. She's a terrific cook. Which reminds me, people keep saying how nice she is and where did I find her, etc. Nothing about how nice I am.

Larry

*

From: Charlie.Dover@duquest.co.co.uk
To: L.Dickerson@verizon.net
19 January 2013

Ooh, poor boy. I think you're nice, though I confess I'm really interested in meeting Melanie.

Doubtless Jewish humour is different here in England.

Charlie

*

From: L.Dickerson@verizon.net
To: Charlie.Dover@duquest.co.uk
January 20, 2013

Dear Charlie

Yeah, and that's not all. It seems Melanie is a second cousin or something to Sandy Koufax. Sandy Koufax! The connection means nothing to you – or for that matter nothing to Melanie – but to me, a baseball fanatic, well you can't imagine. I was able to tell her and the assembled dinner table that Koufax once refused to pitch the first game of a World Series because it was on Yom Kippur. He was not particularly religious; he just thought he shouldn't play baseball on the most sacred day in the Jewish calendar. Koufax was the greatest pitcher of his time, and, according to one very good authority, he was "the smartest pitcher ever." Baseball fans go nuts when they hear this fact about my girlfriend. "Can she get me an autograph?" No, she hasn't seen him in ages.

By the way, I see in the paper that Babe Ruth's baseball jersey sold for 4 million. Four million <u>dollars</u>.

Larry

I'm "collecting" book people here. I told you about Susan Barile, and now I'm back in touch with Julia Rodas, another young woman (almost all women are young to me now), the person who helped me edit and clean up my MacDowell letters for publication. But you are still my favorite pen pal.

From: Charlie.Dover@duquest.co.uk
To: L.Dickerson@verizon.net
21 January 2013

Dear Larry

That's reassuring. I certainly don't want you straying on me. Your girlfriend Melanie is one thing, but two more? And "young women" at that? Besides, there's "Dot" Parker, too.

Yours, worried,
Charlie

CHAPTER NINETEEN

From: L.Dickerson@verizon.net
To: Charlie.Dover@duquest.co.uk
February 3, 2013

Dear Charlie

Jaysus — Osgood delivered once more. I called him some time ago and told him of my new interests. Strangely, I had not been there since moving on to New Yorker writers. You remember how he got three signed Victorian novels for me. On the phone he was most helpful and encouraging as I went into more detail about my new collecting focus. Well, damned if he didn't call me back and say that he had a few inscribed copies of "my" authors. We agreed that I would again bring in my unsigned copies of some of these writers. I was thinking to myself, what would he do with these uninscribed copies if we traded. Maybe he'll just wholesale them out. But I figured that was his problem, not mine. When I brought them in, he just glanced at them quickly.

So I traded in my copy of Mary McCarthy's Memories of a Catholic Girlhood for an inscribed copy — to Harold Ross! Pretty steep at $1,200, but he gave me a 10% discount — as in the past — and then knocked off $400 for my (unsigned) copy, and so $1,080 less $400 equals $680 cash. Then he had a signed Dorothy Parker Laments for the Living also inscribed to Ross. Maybe he got them from someone who bought Ross's library — though if you listen to Brendan Gill, Ross wouldn't have had any books in his house except a few dictionaries. Price was $1,600. With my discount and $300 off for my copy, it came to $1,140. A lot of dough but I just love having books inscribed to Ross.

Next, he showed me an A.J. Liebling, The Sweet Science, inscribed to William Shawn, no less. I didn't have my unsigned copy with me but he said just mail it in. This one was $1,200 minus 10% equals $1,080, minus $300 for my copy, with total cash coming to $780.

He had Mitchell's <u>Up in the Old Hotel</u> inscribed to an unknown, but Irving Gross sent me one of those already.

I saved the best till last – Salinger – can you believe it? Evidently someone got the great recluse to sign a beat-up copy of that dumpy little Signet paperback of <u>Catcher</u> (the one that sold nine million copies):

> For Deborah
> Best regards
> J D Salinger

There is no date. Osgood says he has absolutely no idea who the Deborah is – maybe a playmate or schoolmate of Salinger's daughter. In this case he allowed $330 that I paid for the paperback first Signet, and he gave me this $1,700 item after (my usual) 10% discount, for $1,200. A signed Salinger! Even if it is in a late printing, poor condition, cheap, mass-market paperback.

So, I was pretty overjoyed to leave his shop with four very specially inscribed books. Inscriptions to Ross (two), one to Shawn, and one from Salinger to an unknown "Deborah." Of course I had to lay out a lot of dough. The "list" price on these came to $5,700, but with 10% off the price it comes to $5,130, less $1,330 for my trades. I gave him a check for (only) $3,800. Of course if you count my traded in books, I paid $5,130. In any case, what a day's work. Although I think there is something to be said for getting things like these one at a time, spaced out over time. After all, "The thrill is in the hunt." Buying books up there was good but just a little bit like shooting fish in a barrel. What a network of suppliers he must have. I told him I'd like to find a Nabokov, <u>Speak, Memory</u>, if it were reasonable in price. I nearly said "pricewise" but caught myself.

I realize I am getting terribly (obsessively?) fond of inscribed or signed copies.

Larry

Total outlay to date: $33,435.

Now I am of course dangerously close to the "top" budget of $35,000 – allowing only $5,000 for this year. These signed copies are doing me in. But they are special.

I next stopped by Jim Cummins' place – keeping my Osgood purchases out of sight in a plain paper bag inside my backpack. No use letting him see what I was buying at a rival's. Jaysus, does Cummins have the books. Starting with ancient Bibles at $25,000 and on up through the twentieth century. He had, for $75,000, Catcher in the Rye inscribed to Salinger's would-be mother-in-law (that marriage never happened) and dated December 23, 1951 – year of publication – but it's a Book-of-the-Month Club edition in a "slightly worn dust jacket." Cummins had a Dickens letter for $7,500 (shades of my old days). And he had the damndest Hemingway letter, from 1942, written to his old boxing coach, saying how in his (Hemingway's) living room there at his place in Cuba he boxed 5 one-minute rounds with Hugh Casey. Hugh Casey was a pitcher for the old Brooklyn Dodgers (before my time but still within my range of baseball knowledge). Hemingway doesn't say who won, although he claims he knocked Casey down twice. Price: $12,500.

Cummins had an Oscar Wilde book, The Ballad of Reading Gaol, for a mere $27,500.

Hanging on the wall there's an original Thurber drawing framed – but $7,500 – a lot of money.

I also handled a copy of L. Ron Hubbard's Scientology book, Dianetics, for $450. There is no book in the world that I would rather not have.

*

From: Charlie.Dover@duquest.co.uk
To: L.Dickerson@verizon.net
4 February 2013

Dear Larry

It sounds like you are doing very well. But I definitely again advise you to slow down, take stock. Easy does it.

Charlie

CHAPTER TWENTY

From: Irving.Gross@ns.edu
To: L.Dickerson@verizon.net
February 8, 2013

Dear Larry,

I'm tempted to say, as the youngsters do, "Oh my God," but have you seen the very latest New Yorker? (double issue February 11 and 18)? It contains the long opening section of a memoir by Joseph Mitchell!

Irving

*

From: L.Dickerson@verizon.net
To: Irving.Gross@ns.edu
February 9, 2013

   Haven't seen it yet. My copies have been arriving late, lately.

*

From: Irving.Gross@ns.edu
To: L.Dickerson@verizon.net
February 9, 2013

Dear Larry

For someone like me, who lived for years in the same building with

Mitchell, it's a voice from the past. The piece is called "Street Life: Becoming part of the city." So I, like everybody else, was wrong in believing that Mitchell left nothing publishable behind. He has been dead for 17 years. It's the first chapter of a memoir and is an amazingly introspective account of how he fell in love with New York – all five Boroughs.

Mitchell loved to walk in the city, but he would also spend entire days taking busses to strange places: he would get on a subway train at random; get off at an equally random station, and take the first bus that came in either direction. He would sit in the rear next to a large window so he could look at the streets and the buildings – "the vast, spread-out sooty gray and sooty brown of the horizontal city, the old, polluted, betrayed, and sure-to-be-torn-down-any-time-now city."

We Mitchell devotees should be grateful for anything, but the real tragedy is that he didn't go on with it. Had he continued this memoir, I believe he would have written something that would stand up to the passage of time more so than his journalistic endeavors. But here we have only the long opening chapter, with its last paragraph telling how suddenly he became homesick for his native North Carolina but that when visiting North Carolina he became homesick for New York City; "I was beginning to feel painfully out of place wherever I was." Things in both places seemed to have "gone past" him. Then he recounts how "one Sunday afternoon walking in the ruins of Washington Market, something happened to me that led me, step by step, out of my depression. A change took place in me. And that is what I want to tell you about."

But if this is all we have, we don't know what happened to him. Sad.

Irving

*

From: L.Dickerson@verizon.net
To: Irving.Gross@ns.edu
February 10, 2013

Dear Irving

I'm almost tempted to say, once again, who is gushing now? I have just read the article. Very moving. Christ, I might have overlooked it altogether. Thanks for the information. I think I still lack one or two Mitchell New Yorker books, but they have moved "to the front of the queue" as they say on Netflix.

Larry

*

From: Irving.Gross@ns.edu
To: L.Dickerson@verizon.net
February 10, 2013

Dear Larry

Hold the phone on my lamenting the fact that this article is the entire sum of Mitchell's Memoir to survive. The headnote implies that. But when you go to the "Contributors" page (6) you read that Thomas Kunkel, author of a biography of Harold Ross, has learned of "several chapters of an unfinished memoir." So perhaps there will be more. The same note says Kunkel is writing a biography of Mitchell. I'm going to get in touch with Kunkel.

Irving

I've just read a book called The Receptionist, by Janet Groth, who held that position at The New Yorker for twenty years (she left to become an English professor). She devotes a chapter to Joe Mitchell, whose Friday lunch partner she was over a period of years. She adored him; but quotes him as admitting he had a "graveyard cast of mind."

185

*

From: Irving.Gross@ns.edu
To: L.Dickerson@verizon.net
February 12, 2013

Dear Larry

It seems Tom Kunkel is president of a college in Wisconsin. And he still finds time to write books, and to answer email inquiries. Very kind of him. He tells me that Mitchell left a second chapter (on his North Carolina boyhood), and a third chapter, much shorter, about his falling into a malaise during the late sixties and early seventies, the result of "depression (a family trait), some personal losses, despair over what was happening to NYC at the time, and frustration over his writing paralysis." Kunkel says The New Yorker will probably publish the second chapter sometime next year, but he doesn't know if the magazine will publish the short third chapter. So we don't know what took him out of his malaise – if indeed he did get out of it.

Irving

*

From: L.Dickerson@verizon.net
To: Irving.Gross@ns.edu
February 12, 2013

Dear Irving

   Well, it took them 17 years to get the first part of Mitchell's memoir out, so I wouldn't hold my breath waiting for the next installment.

Larry

CHAPTER TWENTY-ONE

From: L.Dickerson@verizon.net
To: Charlie.Dover@duquest.co.uk
         smeans101@aol.com
February 15, 2013

Dear Charlie and Dear Spencer

I've got a good number of signed or inscribed copies of books — most of them through Phillip Osgood. I also read "The New England Forger" — which scared the daylights out of me. But here's my question for you: Just why is there this enormous difference in dollar values between a perfectly done fake signature or inscription and a real one? Let's use F. Scott Fitzgerald's signature as a hypothetical case. He was signing a stack of twelve of his books (late cheap paperback editions of Gatsby) and falls over dead half way through. The forger then gets hold of the very pen Fitzgerald was using, and the very ink pot, and signs the remaining half dozen books. The forger is so good that no expert can tell the difference. In my hypothetical case, we only know the difference because the first six were seen being signed before the writer keeled over — seen by someone who penciled a little "x" on the last page of each of the first six books. The six faked inscriptions are so good that no one can tell the difference — not Osgood, not Christie's, not Jesus. Why is one from the first six worth $5,000 and the other $5 when nobody can tell the difference? What if no one penciled x's on the first six and all the books got mixed up — then where would we be?

What would an honest dealer do in the latter case (no x's)? Split the difference between $5 and $5,000? and then charge $2,495 while admitting to the potential buyer that the odds are fifty/fifty you bought a real one? Isn't it a little crazy?

Larry

*

From: smeans101@aol.com
To: Dickerson@verizon.net
February 15, 2013

Dear Larry

As your old friend Harold Ross would say, You've got me there.

Spencer

*

From: Charlie.Dover@duquest.co.uk
To: L.Dickerson@verizon.net
16 February 2013

Dear Larry

In the first instance, where the situation is known, the copies with the penciled x's would retain their value, and the others would be worthless in so far as the signatures go.

In the case where the books are unmarked and mixed up? I must say your guess is as good as mine. An honest dealer would probably tell a prospective buyer about the situation, the fifty/fifty odds, as you suggest. The (perhaps forged) books might well become conversation pieces, with the curiosity about the 50/50 chances for authenticity even adding to their eventual value.

If somebody is convinced he or she owns a genuine signature or inscription, let him or her be happy and content with that belief. What you don't know won't hurt you.

188

Collecting can be crazy, as we all agree. The gentle madness thing. And there will always be some element of, let's not call it belief (since that word so troubles you), but trust: trust in people, trust in evidence. Take your great great grandfather's letters: We trusted you; we trusted your story of inheriting the letters; we trusted the evidence of the artifacts themselves. Then in turn buyers trusted Osgood and Christie's because both are believed to be authorities on such matters. On the other hand, there remains the ever so infinitesimally slight a chance that you made the whole business up and had some master forger cook up $400,000 worth of letters by Dickens, Thackeray, et al. But we dismiss such a minuscule chance: we trust the evidence. This any help?

Charlie

*

From: L.Dickerson@verizon.net
To: Charlie.Dover@duquest.co.uk
February 23, 2013

Dear Charlie

Yeah, that's pretty convincing. Thanks for taking all the trouble. Still, my question keeps nagging me. There's probably no completely satisfactory answer – for me at least. So like my hero Harold Ross did when a question got too murky, I'll just say "The hell with it." But again, thanks.

Larry

Mention of hell reminds me of something I was delighted to learn a few days ago: that Mark Twain said how sad it is to think of the numerous Hawaiian Islanders who in times past had gone to their graves in that beautiful place without knowing there was a hell.

CHAPTER TWENTY-TWO

From: Irving.Gross@ns.edu
To: L.Dickerson@verizon.net
February 25, 2013

Dear Larry

Why not read and perhaps collect John Hersey's Hiroshima? It was
published in The New Yorker a year after the war, almost on the
anniversary of the dropping of the atom bomb. Hersey's 30,000-word
article filled up an entire issue of the magazine. No cartoons, nothing else,
except advertisements. Such a move was a real gamble for Ross. He went
back and forth on the idea of a complete issue devoted to a single story
(the idea was Shawn's, as had been the original project of having Hersey
interview Hiroshima victims and tell the story from their viewpoint – "to
wake people up over here").

Once the single issue was agreed upon, Ross, Hersey, and Shawn locked
themselves in Ross's office for two weeks, poring over edits and rewrites.
Ross is on record as having made 200 suggestions. One of his minor
queries entered into New Yorker legend. As Hersey told it, Ross objected
to the word being used to describe damaged bicycles discovered near the
center of the explosion: "Can something two-dimensional be 'lopsided'?"
"Lopsided" was changed to "collapsed." Near total secrecy enveloped the
project as Hersey feverishly rewrote and rewrote.

Ross worried that people who expected and paid for humor (at least in
the cartoons) would feel cheated. He had all newsstand copies carry a
cover warning that this was not the usual issue of The New Yorker,
though it was too late to change the light-hearted cover drawing of people
playing happily in a park.

Ross's worries were completely misplaced: the magazine sold out within hours; scalpers were asking as much as $20 for the 15 cent magazine; requests to reprint poured in; editorials worldwide discussed the article. It was read in its entirety, for four hours, "without commercial interruption," on the ABC Radio Network. The BBC followed suit. Albert Einstein ordered 1,000 reprints (they were unavailable). Alfred A. Knopf rushed to print a book edition, and the Book-of-the-Month Club gave free copies to all its members. Ross wrote to a friend, "I don't think I've ever got as much satisfaction out of anything in my life."

Although the piece started no organized movement, millions of readers became convinced that the bomb should never be used again. In its obituary of Hersey, who died in 1993, The New Yorker claimed, and not without justification, that "Hiroshima" was the most famous magazine article ever published anywhere.

Irving

*

From: L.Dickerson@verizon.net
To: Irving.Gross@ns.edu
February 27, 2013

Dear Irving

    Thanks for all the background. I got an inexpensive copy of Hiroshima and have just read it straight through. A few nights earlier I watched some episodes, including the last one, of Ken Burns' TV documentary, "The War." Christ, you came away from that movie hating the "Nips" and almost regretting you owned a Toyota. But then, two nights later, reading through Hersey in one dose — it's not very long as you know — I couldn't help but admire the Japanese and their heroism after the bombing of Hiroshima. I suppose "stoicism" is a better word.

Larry

191

From: Irving.Gross@ns.edu
To: L.Dickerson@verizon.net
February 27, 2013

Dear Larry

Note that Hersey doesn't do any moralizing; he just lets these six
survivors tell their stories. They somehow become representative of the
100,000 or so killed, and of the deadly illnesses that pursued another
100,000, almost all of them civilians, old men, women, and children. The
penultimate paragraph quotes a Jesuit priest writing to the Vatican saying
that some people regard the bomb as akin to poison gas used against
civilians. Others counter that with the reality of "total war" there was no
difference between civilians and soldiers, and that the bomb served to
warn Japan against further resistance, thereby saving countless lives on
both sides. The paragraph leaves the morality of dropping the bomb open.
Even this ambiguity is presented in the words of another person being
quoted, not through Hersey's own.

Irving

*

From: L.Dickerson@verizon.net
To: Irving.Gross@ns.edu
February 27, 2013

Dear Irving

    Proud to say I didn't have to look up "penultimate" (I looked it up
twice a year ago).
    As for whether we should have dropped the bomb: my father, who
fought in Europe, seldom mentioned the War. But once, when the

question came up about whether we should have dropped the bomb, he got angry. I remember him saying that there was no <u>shred</u> of evidence that anyone "in the whole goddamned country" opposed the bomb at the time. He may have exaggerated, a bit. Ken Burns' account offers the speculative figures that if the bomb had not forced Japan's surrender, invading the Japanese home islands would have cost a million and a half US casualties and five million Japanese casualties. Some people (later) claimed we should have dropped the bomb in some harmless open space to demonstrate to the Japanese what they were up against. But Burns points out that A) we didn't know if the damned thing would work, and B) we only had two bombs. I'm with my old man on this – and with Ken Burns. Of course the whole mess was a hell of a thing, as Harold Ross would say.

I got a pretty good copy of <u>Hiroshima</u> in a dust jacket for only $100 at Left Bank Books.

But then I still called Osgood to keep an eye peeled for a signed <u>Hiroshima</u>, along with a copy of <u>Speak, Memory</u>.

And after much searching on the net, I found a copy of that August 31, 1946 Hiroshima issue of <u>The New Yorker</u>, but at $900 I'm not buying it. I find single back issues of the magazine priced at anywhere from $12,000 for the very first one, down to $5.00 for the very latest. I myself own about 150 of the latest ones.

Larry

Total outlay to date: $33,535

*

From: L.Dickerson@verizon.net
To: Irving.Gross@ns.edu
March 2, 2013

Dear Irving

I was up at Osgood's place again. He just kills me. He told me to bring along my copy of <u>Hiroshima</u>. Son of a gun if he didn't have a nice inscribed copy. I told him I only paid $100 for my unsigned copy. He tells me his copy is a $500 item, but with my discount and allowing $100 on exchange, I could have it for $350. Done, says I.

But there was more to come. Remember that quite some time ago I asked him to find a Nabokov, <u>Speak, Memory</u> for me. In this case I had no trade in, having read the book in that $6 ex-library copy. He explained that what he had was an unimportant later edition but that it was inscribed by the great man himself (to someone neither of us had ever heard of). So I would be paying only for the inscription, really. How much? He says, "Knocking off your discount, let's say $800." Of course I took it.

You won't believe the number of signed <u>New Yorker</u> books I have along with the five signed Victorian books.

                                  Larry

Ross said that while working with Hersey he learned how to pronounce Hiroshima in "a new and fancy way." I'm still not sure how to pronounce it.

Total outlay to date: $34,685.

God almighty, I'm nearing the financial ledge for combined first and second year – already.

CHAPTER TWENTY-THREE

From: L.Dickerson@verizon.net
To: Charlie.Dover@duquest.co.uk
March 2, 2013

Dear Charlie

Christ, a really sad note. I'm feeling pretty depressed. Melanie has
broken up with me, at least for the time being. She thinks I am too
obsessive about book collecting – to the point of neglecting her. And just
a little while ago I thought I – we – were doing so well. I'm sure hoping
this break-up is only temporary. You, as my email lady-friend adviser, are
the only one I can discuss this with, and I really don't know what to say. I
have been trying to get out of books and into the real world more. But
evidently not enough. It really has me down and feeling sorry for myself –
which is stupid, I know. I am usually not a depressed person, but this really
depresses me.

Larry

*

From: Charlie.Dover@duquest.co.uk
To: L.Dickerson@verizon.net
3 March 2013

Dear Larry

I'm truly sorry to hear that you and Melanie broke up. As you say, let's
hope it is only a temporary interruption. It's good of you to confide in me.
There is really little to say except the old bromides. These things happen. If

I were a betting woman, I'd bet you will be back together again before too long. Just show yourself willing to be more flexible. You must learn to compartmentalize your interests – keeping books and collecting in one part of your life and – you know what I mean.

And it's all right to feel sorry and sad. Give in to your feelings. Not that I am any expert.

Charlie

As for being depressed: you may not know but English people are not as keen as are Americans (especially New Yorkers) about seeking professional help, psychotherapy, mood-enhancing drugs, anti-depressants, etc. I'm afraid we are more for trying to pull ourselves up by our own bootstraps. And on this note I remember while at university being given a photocopied page of suggestions by the early 19th century wit and clergyman Sydney Smith. In 1820 he wrote to a lady friend suggesting twenty ways to help assuage "low spirits." I can still remember a handful of them:

See all you can of people you respect and who respect you;

Don't expect too much of life – a sorry business at the best;

Take short views – nothing beyond tea or dinner;

Read amusing books;

Take cool "shower baths";

Be as busy as you can;

Do not endeavor to please everybody to every degree;

Be as much as you can in the open air;

Do not be too severe on yourself, but do yourself justice.

That's all I can remember. Oh, yes, there was something about drinking a
<u>moderate</u> amount of wine. How is that for a 19th-century psychotherapy
program?

*

From: L.Dickerson@verizon.net
To: Charlie.Dover@duquest.co.uk
March 4, 2013

Dear Charlie

    I'm really touched. You said all the right things. And I'll try to be
"cautiously optimistic" about my chances of getting back again with Melanie.
The course of true love doesn't run smoothly, etc.
    As for this Sydney Smith's 20 suggestions against low spirits, you
remembered ten – half of them! First time in my life I've heard something
worthwhile from a clergyman.

Larry

Had to look up "bromides," of course.

*

From: L.Dickerson@verizon.net
To: Charlie.Dover@duquest.co.co.uk
           Irving.Gross@ns.edu
           smeans101@aol.com
March 5, 2013

Dear friends and fellow bookmen – I mean book persons

    A question for you. Who is this Max Beerbohm whose name keeps
cropping up in books about <u>The New Yorker</u>? Despite his being an

197

Englishman and never having written for the magazine, I find that writers keep mentioning him in connection with the magazine: Thurber, Gill, Yagoda, Gopnik, et al. S. N. Behrman (a playwright who had 21 plays on Broadway) wrote a six-part Profile of him in the magazine, and Edmund Wilson, a kind of hot-shot intellectual critic in residence at The New Yorker, said that Beerbohm was "the greatest caricaturist of the kind – that is, portrayer of personalities – in the history of art ." What's more, I've even read that some commentators claim that Beerbohm was really the "first" New Yorker writer — meaning that he was writing like a New Yorker writer before the magazine was founded.

Larry

*　*　*

From:　Irving.Gross@ns.edu
To:　L.Dickerson@verizon.net
March 5, 2013

Dear Larry

Beerbohm is a little out of my range. Of course I know he was a first-rate writer and simultaneously a superb caricaturist, but beyond knowing that, and knowing that Behrman wrote that book about him (it became a Book-of the-Month selection), I am not well read in Beerbohm. Like most other people in my line of work, I'm familiar with his delicious parody of Henry James, and with his one novel, Zuleika Dobson – not a favorite of mine. The notion of his being the "first" New Yorker writer is a stretch.

Your English lady friend at Christie's London will know Beerbohm because he is much better known in England, and his caricatures are auctioned in London by both Christie's and Sotheby's. So if you are really interested in writer-artists, Beerbohm comes quickly to mind, along with William Blake, D. G. Rossetti, and, to a lesser degree, Thackeray; and of course your friend Thurber.

Irving

From: Charlie.Dover@duquest.co.co.uk
To: L.Dickerson@verizon.net
6 March 2013

Dear Larry

You can't go wrong with Max Beerbohm. And his prices, given his high reputation (but only among the elect), put him within your collecting range.

Charlie

From: smeans101@aol.com
To: L.Dickerson@verizon.net
March 7, 2013

Dear Larry

Yes, Beerbohm has been one of my collecting specialties. Here's what I recommend. Get a paperback called The Incomparable Max, a collection of his writings; this will give you an idea of his prose. Then get a second-hand copy, still not cheap, of Nathan Halderin's Max Beerbohm Caricatures. With these two books you can see whether you like his writings and drawings. Everyone likes the drawings. Whenever a publication like The New York Review of Books reviews a book on Henry James, Rossetti, Shaw, Yeats, or a dozen others, they print a Beerbohm drawing to accompany the review. Recently the NYRB reproduced his perhaps most famous caricature, "Rossetti in His Back Garden," and they have made a hash of identifying the model, who is obviously not Lizzie Siddal, but Fanny Cornforth, plump and bosomy and Rossetti's mistress and model. Lizzie Siddal was thin and ethereal and <u>dead</u> before Rossetti acquired the Chelsea house with the famous backyard. It's disgusting when you know something about a subject and see it mangled in the press. Pardon my wrath. I enclose a scan of the caricature.

Beerbohm lived to be an old man, dying age 84 in 1956. Yet he was well known back in the 1890s and was a friend of all the members of the Oscar Wilde circle, that is, not just Wilde himself, but Robert Ross, Reggie Turner, Frank Harris, G. B. Shaw, and many others. And he <u>drew</u> all of these "personages" (as he called them) in so distinctive a manner that many people today remember these worthies chiefly as seen through Max's drawings (we in the know only use his first name, as did he in signing his work).

Tell me what you think, having looked into those two books.

Spencer

*

From: L.Dickerson@verizon.net
To: smeans101@aol.com
March 10, 2013

Dear Spencer

   I'm hooked, certainly on the caricatures. I'm furthering my reading of the prose – especially the short stories in <u>Seven Men</u>.

                                                                Larry

                              * * *

From: Charlie.Dover@duquest.co.uk
To: L.Dickerson@verizon.net
18 March 2013

Dear Larry

I should have mentioned to you that you might start with Max Beerbohm's most well-known book, his only novel, <u>Zuleika Dobson</u>. Then work backwards (before you run out of money) on to the slight books <u>More</u>, <u>The Happy Hypocrite</u>, and his first book, which had the jokey title <u>The Works of Max Beerbohm</u>, a little collection of essays published when he was 23. The publication of this first book dealt, Max said, "a near fatal blow to my modesty."

Charlie

When women started attending Oxford or Cambridge in numbers, as in my case, it used to be said that every young woman arriving at her college thought of herself as a sort of Zuleika Dobson – a beautiful woman in what was still a man's world. Of course nobody committed suicide over me.

*

From: L.Dickerson@verizon.net
To: Charlie.Dover@duquest.co.uk
March 19, 2013

Dear Charlie

I've seen the name, Zuleika Dobson, because it was number 59 on the list of 100 best English language novels of the 20th century. I am reading the paperback. Takes a little catching on, but once you do, it's not bad.

I bet there were a few who nearly did themselves in for you.

I took a copy of Zuleika Dobson from James Cummins – $400. He showed me some Beerbohm-related stuff, including expensive Oscar Wilde books.

Then I walked over to Osgood's place to tell him I had added Max Beerbohm to my collecting list, and damned if he didn't have an inscribed book. And I bought it. He's a real salesman. It was not as dear as I thought it would be. It's a copy of Yet Again inscribed to Bohun Lynch (I find this Bohun – what a name – Lynch later wrote a biography of Max). The inscription is on the half title – which I have learned is the page just before the real title page. Here Max has doctored the page, employing the printed title into his inscription. Very clever.

This was $425, inscribed. Max Beerbohm is not an expensive author to collect, or so it seems. I have my eye on a boxed set of Works and More. That will leave me missing only The Happy Hypocrite among his earliest prose books. These would put me past my budget. Of course one side of me says stop here; the other says $35,000 is an artificial barrier, so why be bound by it.

Larry

I must share this with you. Last night I read quickly a good deal of one of my favorites, "Dot" Parker. In this case it was Constant Reader, which reprints her early New Yorker book reviews. She thought Hemingway was the best short story writer until she read Max Beerbohm's Seven Men!

202

Parker adored the stories of Ring Lardner: "It is difficult to review these spare and beautiful stories; it would be difficult to review the Gettysburg address."

But most of the reviews were put-downs. Aimee Semple McPherson, the famous lady preacher, tent-revivalist, and faith-healer, is "Our Lady of the Loudspeaker."

Her review of Theodore Dreiser opens with the question, "What writes worse than a Theodore Dreiser?" Some say "Two Theodore Dreisers," while others "rejoice at the merciful absurdity of the conception."

Yale Professor William Lyon Phelps' small book Happiness is "second only to a rubber duck as the ideal bathtub companion."

Parker begins her review of The Autobiography of Margot Asquith with a child asking his daddy what an optimist is. Daddy says, "One who thought Margot Asquith wasn't going to write any more."

Total outlay to date: $35,510!

OK, so much for only 5K this year.

CHAPTER TWENTY-FOUR

From: L.Dickerson@verizon.net
To: Irving.Gross@ns.edu
April 15, 2013

Dear Irving

    Just reporting in. What a book weekend I had! At Susan Barile's urging I went to <u>two</u> book fairs – the first time I go to any book fair and I end up at two of them in two days.

    As you know, the Annual Antiquarian Book Fair at the Park Avenue Armory held this last weekend is a very big deal. This fair is for the luxury book sellers, high-end, or whatever you want to call it. But the small-time booksellers hold a "shadow" book fair on West 18th Street, and Susan herself had a booth there. The big boys up at 66th Street can come downtown and buy up the creme. I went Friday evening to this smaller event, knowing the prices would be smaller too. Most of the books were within my budget although they did not have much in the way of what I am collecting. There was for example a "heavily foxed" Dickens' <u>Dombey and Son</u> rebound for only $450. I can hear Spencer saying "Condition, condition, condition." Besides, I am out of my Victorian phase, although I like to keep an eye on things from that time. So I got out without buying anything. Are you proud of me? I saw a copy of Joseph Mitchell's <u>Up In the Old Hotel</u>. Someone wanted $1,400 for a signed copy – the very same item you sent me gratis. But you are too much a gentleman to ask for it back.

Larry

*

From: Irving.Gross@ns.edu
To: L.Dickerson@verizon.net
April 16, 2013

Dear Larry

$1,400 for that book seems very dear. And yes, if you weren't such a good pal I'd tell you to sell the copy I gave you and then pay me half. But being as you are such a nice guy I will suggest nothing of the kind. Moreover, you wouldn't be able to sell it at that price; only a big-time dealer, a dealer "to the carriage trade," could ask such a price for that book.

Go ahead and tell me about the Armory prices. I know you are dying to shock me.

Irving.

*

From: L.Dickerson@verizon.net
To: Irving.Gross@ns.edu
April 16, 2013

Dear Irving

    Well, ok, if you insist. But even the setting can knock your socks off — a cliche, sorry. I spent all Saturday afternoon in the huge old Park Avenue Armory. As you know, it takes up an entire city block and is a national landmark. After you pay your $20 for a single day ticket you enter a sea of identical small spot lights shining down on hundreds of white booths. Now these hundreds of booths are all of them identical, having counters with glass fronts and tops, and display book cases with sliding glass doors. The only difference between them is in size and location. I know this because I called the ABAA and asked what it costs to have a booth at this particular vanity fair. It depends on size and location, $7,000 to $12,000 — so you can see that a dealer has to sell some pretty expensive things to break even – which they obviously do. I was a little shy at first but then I got to chatting with a few dealers. Jim Cummins I of course knew and he was very cordial. I also talked to David Bauman and told him I was a novice collector of modest means and that I had once bought a book at his place. He urged me to come in and look at any time. Besides his New York Madison Avenue location he has another place in Philadelphia and for the last half dozen years or so another one in Las Vegas, and – get this – they have more customers coming into the Las Vegas place than into the other two stores combined. I don't know what that says.

Then I talked with the Boston dealer Peter Stern, who had a copy of The Return of the Native, original bindings and signed by Hardy; but in spite of a "small W H Smith library blind stamp and only trivial foxing," the price was $85,000!

At a booth specializing in autographs, I asked the owner – whose name I forget – if he knew Phillip Osgood and if he had a booth (actually I knew damn well from the program that Osgood did not have a booth). This fellow says, "Yes I know him, and No he is not exhibiting at this fair." Very curt about it he was, and then he looked away and busied himself with some papers. Fircrissakes, I realize Osgood must be his direct competitor, but that was no reason for him to be so short with me.

Ok. So as not to bore your head off, I'll just mention a few of the prices. Dickens, Oliver Twist, 3 volumes, in original cloth for $17,000; an autograph Dickens letter mentioning the American Civil War – $15,000; David Copperfield in monthly parts, $20,000.

Oh, and of course Darwin. On the Origin, a true first, one of those 1,250 copies from 1859, can be yours for $225,000.

Then, get this, a striking photograph of Charles Darwin with his great beard for $195,000. (I am trying not to use the exclamation point for extra emphasis.) The dealer instructed me that this photo is by a famous Victorian photographer, Julia Margaret Cameron, and it is signed by Darwin, and is one of only three known copies of this photograph. OK, all important factors, but still, that's 195 thousand. Talk about "carriage trade."

I got talking with a very friendly London dealer, Ed Maggs, who relayed to me a well-known bit of book collecting wisdom, namely that every collector should have three copies of his books. The first for his collection, the second for his own reading, and a third for lending to friends. It seems that people who are scrupulously honest in most things think nothing about not bothering to return a book lent to them. Maggs showed me some wonderful drawings – portraits – one of Yeats (about whom I know nothing) that he just sold to a man named Mark Samuels Lasner. He asked if I knew him – he said everyone in the book business knows this Mark fellow. Maybe someday.

Now, for my current real collecting interest, that is New Yorker authors, there was not too much. Although I did see a Dorothy Parker book I never heard of, After Such Pleasures, 1933, "near fine," in dust jacket, for $150. Must have been the least expensive thing in the whole show. And I bought it.

As for Nabokov: the same Peter Stern had the Paris first edition of Lolita for $7,500 – in "near fine" condition. I've seen it advertised for $10,000.

Of course there was Salinger, most notably a copy of Catcher in the Rye, a true first, and featuring the explanation that five generations of collectors may have been duped into thinking they had first printing dust jackets when they were second printings. Something unintelligible to me about a line above the headshot on the back cover, a line "not visible to the naked eye." $20,000.

Then there were the books I keep an eye on just because of their demand: Ulysses, a true first, etc, was $225,000. The other book I keep an eye on is The Great Gatsby: a copy without a dust jacket was $5,500. A copy with "chipped dust jacket and professional repair" was $180K. Less than I expected. It must depend on just what "repair" means here. Even the goddam later Modern Library edition of Gatsby is $5,500.

Oscar Wilde is very expensive, his inscribed books going for $75,000. Had enough?

Larry

Oh yes, Dr Seuss, The Cat in the Hat, first edition, $9,000; Beatrix Potter, Peter Rabbit, a first edition is $105,000. Did I mention F. Scott Fitzgerald's walking stick for $75,000?

Total outlay to date: $35,660.

This is $660 past my absolute tops for the time being.

From: L.Dickerson@verizon.net
To: SusanBarile1.@yahoo.com
April 16, 2013

Dear Susan

   I am sending you a copy of my latest email to Irving Gross, recounting my adventures at the book fairs you encouraged me to attend. The prices at the Armory amaze me. Phillip Osgood did not have a booth. Actually, I was just as glad he was not there. He's the guy who paid me a great deal of money for those old letters, and from whom I have bought a good number of great inscribed books, but I feel uneasy with him. I kind of see myself as flying under false colors when dealing with him. That is, he sort of intimidates me. I guess in plain English I would say that I don't particularly like him. Neither does my lady friend at Christie's London, but she says this is no reason not to trust him professionally.

   If going to that Fair among all those hundreds of dealers meant anything to me, it was to make me know my place in the book collecting universe, which is pretty low down on the scale.

   But thanks "irregardless," as the kids say, for encouraging me to go to both fairs.

                                        Larry

                    *

From: SusanBarile1.@yahoo.com
To: L.Dickerson@verizon.net
April 17, 2013

Hi Larry

Thanks for all the "dope" on the Armory show. But, Larry, please stop putting yourself down. You are a mid-range collector. And in the past, the very recent past – have you already forgotten? – you owned $400,000 worth of really spectacular letters from Dickens, George Eliot, Thackeray, Trollope, Hardy, etc. Many of those dealers haven't anything like that to offer. Moreover, you published your edition of those letters. How many of them have published much more than catalogues and book lists?

Susan

*

From: L.Dickerson@verizon.net
To: SusanBarile1@yahoo.com
April 17, 2013

Dear Susan

   I suppose the truth is that at first I had no idea how special those Victorian letters were. And then once I did realize what they really were, the shock was not so great because I had had them around so long. Well, it was a nice shock. And it is goddam nice of you to send me such an encouraging email.

                                        Larry

CHAPTER TWENTY-FIVE

From: Kimherzinger@gmail.com
To: L.Dickerson@verizon.net
April 18, 2013

Dear Larry

From deep in the heart of Texas I say hello and also send some very strange news. We discussed Phillip Osgood when we spoke some months ago. You told me how you had sold that wonderful collection of your great great grandfather's correspondence to him for $400,000 (and worth every penny of it), and how you were now buying inscribed books from him from time to time. I mentioned that Osgood drops by our shop every once in a while and buys a handful of books. I have always wondered about this because the books he gets from me are usually not in prime condition and not inscribed – inscriptions being a sideline of his autograph specialty. Well, listen to this. Osgood is being investigated by the federal prosecutor's NY office for forged signatures and consumer fraud across state lines. I hate to be the messenger, but I decided I should send you a heads-up. Although I am certainly a small, "down town" bookseller, I have friends among the big guys, and one of them told me about Osgood.

I have no idea whether any of the inscribed books which you bought from Osgood are bad or not; he certainly deals as much in genuine materials as forged inscriptions, if indeed he does knowingly sell phony inscriptions, because at this point it's only an allegation. But I'm told the feds don't bother bringing a case unless they are pretty damn sure there is something wrong going on. In any event, I thought I'd email you from here because I won't be back in the shop till June 1. Actually, I feel a bit guilty about not mentioning the suspicions about Osgood earlier. But even to hint at such a thing about a book dealer is a serious matter. Once the word "bad" books or "forged inscriptions" gets around, there's no retreat, really, even if the accusation is unfounded or if the dealer acted in good faith. It's a little like accusing someone of plagiarism. Once the charge is made, the accused, innocent or not, is going to suffer under it. So I hesitated to mention this rumor to you when we were talking. I did say he was a "slick" talker, but that is hardly a crime. Perhaps you should just sit tight and see what comes of all this.

Kim

*

From: L.Dickerson@verizon.net
To: Kimherzinger@gmail.com
April 18, 2013

Dear Kim

Christ, that's a heads up all right! I hardly know what to do.

Larry

*

From: Kimherzinger@gmail.com
To: L.Dickerson@verizon.net
April 19, 2013

Dear Larry

As I said, I can't presume to advise you. Osgood obviously deals in many authentic items, for instance, your MacDowell letters, so you don't know if your inscribed books are bad or the real thing. When I learn more about Osgood, I'll email you.

Word gets around quickly in the book world. Everybody will know about the investigation of Osgood in no time.

I expect other dealers who have bought things from Osgood will now think about questioning the books they got from him and come forward. It could be a real mess, especially if the fraud is widespread and the books were dispersed to other dealers or clients. But again of course at this point it is only an investigation, and we don't know the real state of things.

Kim

* * *

From: L.Dickerson@verizon.net
To: Charlie.Dover@duquest.co.uk
April 19, 2013

Dear Charlie — and tell this to Stephen, forward it to him.

Phillip Osgood, who paid me $400,000 for my MacDowell letters, is under investigation for fraud! By the Feds. Kim Herzinger of Left Bank Books emailed me with a heads up. Herzinger knew about my selling the MacDowell letters to Osgood (I told him, of course) and also that I was buying books from Osgood. Jesus, does this implicate me? They can't get at my money can they? Herzinger says "everybody" will know about this in no time, it'll be the "talk of the (book) town."

What do I do? I wonder if I should contact the prosecutor.

Larry

*

From: Charlie.Dover@duquest.co.uk
To: L.Dickerson@verizon.net
20 April 2013

Dear Larry

We have just heard of the investigation. There's no problem here for you.
You don't have to do anything. I'd recommend you simply wait and see
what develops. Try not to worry: We do know that your MacDowell
letters have a rock-solid provenance. As for the inscribed books you
bought from him, that may be a different matter. Tell me titles and prices.

Charlie

*

From: L.Dickerson@verizon.net
To: Charlie.Dover@duquest.co.uk
April 20, 2013

Dear Charlie

My inscribed books from Osgood are:

    Thackeray, Vanity Fair, $4,500
    Trollope, Orley Farm, $4,000
    Butler, Erewhon, $800
    Liebling, The Sweet Science, $1,180.
    McCarthy, Memories of a Catholic Girlhood, $1,080.
    Parker, Laments for the Living, $1,440.
    Salinger, Catcher in the Rye, paperback, $1,530.
    Beerbohm, Yet Again, $425.
    Nabokov, Speak, Memory, $600
    Hersey, Hiroshima, $500.

Ten titles. Three Victorians, six <u>New Yorker</u> writers, and one Beerbohm. They come to $16,055 (I didn't realize I spent so much money at Osgood's). My discount of 10% is reflected in these totals (the Salinger, for example, was "listed" at $1,700). But I laid out only $11,355 in cash because I got credit of $4,700 for the six unsigned books I traded in.

Larry

*

From: Charlie.Dover@duquest.co.uk
To: L.Dickerson@verizon.net
23 April 2013

Dear Larry

Thanks for the list. My first inclination was to think that in fact you may have paid too little for these books, which could indicate a problem. On the other hand, if the books themselves were in less than good condition or not "true firsts," then the prices are reasonably fair, and you would pretty much be paying just for the signatures, a little on the low side, but not outrageously so (which would be a bad sign).

Please try to relax, my friend. This, too, will pass.

Charlie

*

From: L.Dickerson@verizon.net
To: Charlie.Dover@duquest.co.uk
April 23, 2013

Dear Charlie

I am trying to relax. But, as you probably know, I'm something of a worrier. And even though I know damn well that I did nothing wrong, I don't like the fact that the man who paid me nearly half a million dollars is under criminal investigation. I know it's not as if I had money from Bernie Madoff – or worse yet, had given Madoff my $400,000 to invest, in which case I wouldn't be buying books today.

The books I bought from Osgood seemed to me to be in decent, but not great condition. (Although, remember that Spencer Means told Gross I was not careful enough about condition.) I thought these books were good buys but certainly not "steals," if I can use that word here. Perhaps this was wishful thinking on my part.

I called Spencer Means, and on the provenance issue he pointed out that he himself has many inscribed copies in his collection. He has reason to believe that all his inscribed books are genuine – but it's almost impossible to be absolutely sure unless, for example, the provenance can be traced back to the very person it was inscribed to. As he explained it, if there was a sale, for example, of Somerset Maugham's library, held immediately after his death, and a book turns up in it inscribed to Maugham, you can be pretty sure that the inscription is genuine. Unless of course Somerset Maugham himself was a forger.

Means was non-committal about whether I should call the cops, that is, the prosecutor, or maybe have the signatures checked by some other well-known autograph specialist – or just sit tight and see what happens. Because of course I don't at this point know if my signed copies are forgeries or not – so what business have I got calling the prosecutor when I don't know where I stand in all this?

Means checked out Osgood for me, and found that Osgood is not a member of the Antiquarian Booksellers Association of America. Of course membership is voluntary, but it involves nomination by two member dealers and then careful vetting. Spencer also tells me that Osgood is not a member of the Grolier Club, the New York club for (primarily well-to-do) collectors and dealers. Here again you can't just "join," you have to be nominated by two members and be voted on by the membership committee. Naturally, there is no law saying anyone must join any organization. It's just that you would <u>think</u> that such a high-end dealer in New York City would be a member of both the ABAA and the Grolier Club. So a negative take on the situation would say that Osgood may have come up short of ABAA standards and may have been blackballed at the Grolier. Just speculation, but here are two <u>possible</u> bad signs.

This also explains why Osgood did not exhibit at the big Antiquarian Book Fair here – you have to be a member of the ABAA.

Larry

PS In the back of my mind, I have my eye on – is that a mixed metaphor? – a fairly good size original water-color Beerbohm caricature. It's similar to the famous "Rossetti in His Back Garden" caricature. Perhaps it's even a study for that drawing – with figures of Morris, Swinburne, Ruskin, et al. Expensive, of course. But the worry over Osgood keeps pushing this – and everything else – out of my mind.

From: Charlie.Dover@duquest.co.uk
To: L.Dickerson@verizon.net
26 April 2013

Dear Larry

I almost hesitate to tell you this, but the antiquarian book world is a close-knit and gossipy place, and word gets around very quickly. By now everybody knows of the charges against Osgood. Therefore I think I should tell you, although it need not concern you, and I really mean this, but two of our clients, both Americans, have written independently asking about the authenticity of their purchases here at Christie's: one of them

216

bought your Dickens letters, and the other bought your Hardy letters. Both buyers knew that we were auctioning them for Osgood, and that he in turn got them from you. I wrote to these clients assuring them of the authenticity of the letters. Our legal team is doing likewise.

No cause for worry. Go back to collecting.

Charlie

*

From: L.Dickerson@verizon.net
To: Charlie.Dover@duquest.co.uk
April 26, 2013

Dear Charlie

    I wish to hell I had a goddam "legal team." Sure, we are sure about the provenance of those letters. But it's no fun having your name mixed up with somebody who looks like a swindler. And it's also no fun thinking that my precious inscriptions may be forgeries.

Larry

*   *   *

From: Kimherzinger@gmail.com
To: L.Dickerson@verizon.net
May 1, 2013

Dear Larry

My confidant now has told me just how Osgood got caught. And it isn't just Osgood – he's been working with a fly-by-night dealer by the name of

217

Charles Nevins. This Nevins is a small-time seller who for a few years worked out of Santa Cruz, California. He kept changing the name of his shop, and at least a few rumors surfaced that he was selling bad inscriptions. But no one called him on it. The forgery remained only a rumor. We should keep in mind that really desirable books, especially inscribed ones, pass around among dealers and often do so quickly. But dealers, being human, are often sucked in. If some small fish offers a big time dealer a glowing inscription from Hemingway to Fitzgerald, the big time dealer will want to believe it's genuine, especially if he has already as good as sold the book to a wealthy client at a price four or six (or more) times what he paid Nevins for the book. It would take a really conscientious dealer, on the basis of a rumor alone, to think about investigating and then recalling a book he has already sold to a client for a very substantial profit. Dealers in California and in other states were getting suspicious books from Nevins, and most dealers just sent them back – after all, Nevins bought them from someone so maybe he was an innocent party. Some unscrupulous dealers, despite the rumors, probably did not return them but kept and resold them. You can hear one of these dealers saying, "You buy used books 'as is,' and you sell books 'as is,' so it's let the buyer beware." Maybe the more honest dealers who simply returned the books to Nevins should have done more. I suppose most people don't like to "make waves."

Well, Nevins relocated to Bergen County, New Jersey, near New York City, a year or two ago – calling himself Firstbooks. The talk is now that Nevins was in fact the forger, and that Osgood was his partner in crime. Osgood was not just some big time dealer who was duped by Nevins: he was in cahoots with him, sending him unsigned copies and "commissioning" signatures and inscriptions. In fact, I bet Osgood sent him some of those (uninscribed) books purchased from me!

So both Osgood and Nevins are now indicted, and not only for fraud but for conspiracy.

My same pal on the Upper East Side told me how they finally got the goods on Osgood and Nevins. One prominent dealer in New York, Harris

Strock, received a request from Nevins for a book on his recent list. The book was Joyce's Portrait of the Artist, an unjacketed second edition, Egoist Press, 1917. Strock, while packing up the book to send it to Nevins, remembering the rumor about bad books coming from him, decides "just for the hell of it" (as he later said) to put a little penciled circle around the page number on page 16 of the book. I wonder if Strock had read and remembered the Goldstones' Warmly Inscribed with its vivid account of how the New England Forger was caught. In any case, Strock, sometime later, was talking with a fellow dealer at the Grolier Club, who tells Strock he had purchased from Osgood a 1917 edition of Portrait of the Artist inscribed by Joyce to his lifelong friend Claud Sykes. This dealer has the book on offer at a rather spectacular price. "When you go into your shop tomorrow," Strock tells his bookseller friend, "Look at page 16 and see if there is a penciled circle around that number." It became an "Ah hah" moment. The proverbial you-know-what hit the fan. Inquiries followed. Osgood is shown to have received that book and many others from Nevins. In fact I am quite sure some of the books Osgood purchased from me are now signed or inscribed and resting with collectors or other dealers. For all we know some of the books you used as trade-ins with Osgood may have become valuable inscribed association copies.

Exciting times, right?

Kim

*

From: L.Dickerson@verizon.net
To: Kimherzinger@gmail.com
May 1, 2013

Dear Kim

Christ, thanks for the scoop on Osgood. I'm still dithering about whether I should contact the authorities about my Osgood books. I keep hoping mine are genuine inscriptions.

I'm going to forward your email to my woman friend at Christie's London, who has been sort of holding my hand through all this.

Larry

* * *

From: L.Dickerson@verizon.net
To: Charlie.Dover@duquest.co.uk
May 1, 2013

Dear Charlie

Listen to this! I am forwarding to you my email from Kim Herzinger. Now Osgood has been INDICTED – no longer just being investigated. This Charles Nevins character also.

Larry

*

From: L.Dickerson@verizon.net
To: Charlie.Dover@duquest.co.uk
May 2, 2013

Dear Charlie

Jesus Christ almighty. Can you believe this? An FBI agent was just at the door asking me if I would voluntarily come down to talk with the prosecutor about this Osgood case. Even I knew from the movies that I should say that I must check first with a lawyer. So here I was, wondering if I should contact the authorities about the books I bought from Osgood, and then they show up before I can make up my goddam mind. Now of course I wish to hell I had contacted the authorities two weeks ago when

220

Kim Herzinger told me about Osgood. But, as I keep saying, I am still not sure mine are among the fake signatures.

The agent asked if I would voluntarily send them all the inscribed books that I bought from Osgood – send them before our meeting, if we do meet. I said I would talk to my lawyer on this also.

The FBI agent implied that if I refused to come in, the prosecutor could have me subpoenaed to a grand jury!

God. My hands are shaking as I type this although I know I am as innocent as the day is long (cliche?). I will check with Melanie, who seems to know a lot of lawyers.

Larry

*

From: L.Dickerson@verizon.net
To: Charlie.Dover@duquest.co.uk
May 2, 2013

Charlie

Sorry to write again. I called Melanie and left an urgent message on the answering machine. I was still in a state of shock. In the elevator, two of my neighbors asked me why I looked so distracted. So I briefly told them about the Osgood situation. Well, when we got downstairs, one of these neighbors, a really swell black guy who lives in the building – his name is Franklin – hangs around to talk to me. "So," he says, "you got arrested." This is a kind of half joke, but this Franklin seems to know a lot about cops and arrests, etc. So I decided to tell him about the situation in a little more detail, and then he says, "Watch out, and don't let them send a car for you. If you get in their car, you are under arrest!" Franklin – who years ago had a scrape with the law – says the cops would like to arrest everybody. If two people are completely independently suspected in the same crime, the police would just as well have <u>both</u> of them put in jail. He says that from what I told him, the Feds may think I am a co-conspirator, a receiver or

221

distributor of fraudulent goods. I told him, Christ, I did absolutely nothing wrong. But Franklin says (pardon the word, but it's a direct quote), "Cops don't give a shit if you did anything wrong, they just want to get you convicted." I realize Franklin has a very unfavorable view of law enforcement. But on the other hand, he seems to know what he is talking about. So I asked him if he thinks I need a lawyer, and he says, "You're damn right you need a lawyer. Don't agree to anything or say boo to anybody without a lawyer by your side." Franklin knows of one prosecutor in New Jersey who bragged, "I can indict anyone. I could indict a ham sandwich."

Larry

*

From: L.Dickerson@verizon.net
To: Charlie.Dover@duquest.co.uk
May 2, 2013

Dear Charlie

My third email today. I called Melanie again and told her about this. I think she felt sorry for me and wants me to come up to her place tonight, so that at least is good news. It's an ill wind that doesn't do some good, right? I'm ready to "come forward" but don't even know how. Melanie will give me the name of a lawyer who is a right fit – she will get a recommendation from a divorce lawyer she knows very well. I don't want to be spending money on lawyers' fees when the money could be buying me that Rossetti caricature. But it can't be helped. God, how did I get involved?

Larry

*

From: Charlie.Dover@duquest.co.uk
To: L.Dickerson@verizon.net
5 May 2013

Dear Larry

Sorry, I've been away a few days. Larry, besides a lawyer you have something else on your side, viz., the fact that <u>you haven't done anything wrong</u>. You probably should have contacted the authorities, and our advice to you to sit tight was probably wrong. But that's past changing. You are in no way compromised by all this. My thinking is you will eventually get your money back.

Charlie

*

From: L.Dickerson@verizon.net
To: Charlie.Dover@duquest.co.uk
May 6, 2013

Dear Charlie

    <u>Of course</u> I know that I did nothing wrong.
    I met with my lawyer (a nice, smart guy, and Jewish, thank God), and he explained that he would speak with the prosecutor to find out exactly what the case is against Osgood and exactly what my standing is in all this, including of course the question of why they would like to speak with me. And although the lawyer's language was less salty than my friend Franklin's, he did warn me that the U S Attorney's Office has a reputation for "dogged determination" in getting indictments. He said that if they really have me in mind as a "possible suspect" and in any way act on it, this would not be the first incident of "prosecutorial misconduct" that he has dealt with. You can imagine how delighted I was to hear that.

223

He said he would send my Osgood books to the Prosecutor's Office.

Larry

*

From: L.Dickerson@verizon.net
To: Charlie.Dover@duquest.co.uk
May 9, 2013

Dear Charlie

Christ, the plot thickens. This lawyer of mine, John Reiner, visited the prosecutor about my case. He confirmed that yes, there were two book sellers who presented the prosecutor with enough evidence that Osgood and Nevins were dealing in forgeries for the prosecutor to pursue a criminal case. Now other dealers are coming forward. Apparently the sales of books from Osgood to these dealers involved very high prices — way out of my league. Of course if these book dealers were such smart big-time booksellers, you would think they would have had enough experience to not have bought the books from Osgood in the first place.

But the real shocker is this: The prosecutor, who was able to subpoena Osgood's financial books, found the $400,000 paid to me for "manuscript letters" about four years ago; and then he also saw various sales of inscribed books sold to me (much less expensive but still real money). So he wanted to talk with me about both selling the letters and buying the books. The prosecutor said that it's possible I could be simply a victim (assuming my books are "bad"). But he also thought that it was possible I could be involved in a conspiracy to sell fraudulent goods! He would like to speak with me, if I am willing. If not, he will subpoena me. At this point I am nearly going crazy. The lawyer urged calm and said that we should voluntarily talk with the prosecutor, and that by our "performance" and documentation we would "easily" demonstrate my status as a victim only. It was helpful that we have already sent my books down in evidence. I said that the mere fact of their suspecting me makes it sound like we are living

in a police state. And he said, very coolly, "My dear friend, we <u>are</u>. But you will be altogether cleared – and you may even get some money back."
The prosecutor is having my books independently evaluated, and preliminary findings point to most of the inscriptions being fakes. So all my worrying was not just foolish anxiety on my part, after all. Sure I'm completely innocent, but they have suspicions – or at least "avenues" they wish to explore. I just wish that I was not one of those avenues. The advice that I didn't need a lawyer was just plain wrong. Not that I'm bragging about worrying so much, but still, there it is.

Of course now I <u>really</u> wish I had joined the investigation against Osgood back when Herzinger reported him being under suspicion – but then again as I keep saying and telling myself, I had no proof that my books were bad, until now, when I find out indirectly via my lawyer. I was always <u>hoping</u> mine were authentic signatures. My sending these books down to the prosecutor happened, as you know, only when I was asked to "voluntarily" do so and as Reiner advised. But doing this so late in the game is a little like joining the parade after the damn thing is nearly over. (Mixed metaphor.)

Larry

Trollope in <u>Orley Farm</u> mentions the "terrible meshes of the law." Now I know what he means.

From: Charlie.Dover@duquest.co.uk
To: L.Dickerson@verizon.net
11 May 2013

Dear Larry

I can understand how troublesome all this is. I am truly sorry that you have to go through all this stress. But what is it now, only two days till you see the prosecutor? You will have your lawyer with you, and it will be shown that you are in no way implicated in any wrongdoing.

Then you should go out and buy that expensive Beerbohm/Rossetti caricature you were thinking about just before all this happened. Go ahead and splurge! You should have at least one spectacular drawing to complement your book collection.

And in due course let's hope you will get an additional Beerbohm drawing or two when they come up for auction here. You must come over to London. Think positive.

Your friend
Charlie

*

From: L.Dickerson@verizon.net
To: Charlie.Dover@duquest.co.uk
May 13, 2013

Dear Charlie

I'm back from the prosecutor's office. You were right, but only in part. Tell Stephen. Here's a report for you, the kindest of my advisers.

We met, my lawyer and I and the prosecutor and the FBI agent. In regard to my letters and the $400,000, Christ, they wouldn't even let me tell them the whole story. (My lawyer told me beforehand that unless he interrupted I should do the talking.) Well, I barely got started on the old Victorian letters when the prosecutor announced that Christie's legal people had answered a "private communication" from the prosecutor's office about those letters just this morning. (Evidently even you were not yet notified.) No criminal dealings involved. That part of the investigation is closed, period. I got the sense that the authorities were <u>really</u> <u>disappointed</u>. The amount of money in that transaction was a hell of a lot more than the combined sums I paid Osgood for the inscribed books.

So, next we moved right on to the inscribed books that I bought from Osgood. There were my ten books, stacked up on a desk. The prosecutor produced a report from an independent handwriting expert that said in his opinion all the signatures except one were forgeries. Moreover, all these books except one had come to Osgood from Nevins! The prosecutor said he would read only one brief comment from this report, namely that "The total of $1,700 for any edition of Catcher in the Rye inscribed by Salinger was woefully underpriced, and that such underpricing can often point to the seller's desiring to 'unload' a counterfeited inscription." The prosecutor looks up at me and says, "Didn't you think that $1,700 was too much of a bargain for that book?" So I say, "When someone in the know, someone like Osgood, offers you something you would love to own, you would not be the first person to start complaining that the price is too low."

I then asked the prosecutor which signature the expert found genuine, and it turned out to be Beerbohm's inscription to the book Yet Again. Here once more the prosecutor referred to the expert's report that "not only did this handwriting appear genuine, but the inscription itself was probably too clever for any forger to have made up" (remember how Beerbohm had incorporated the printed half title into the inscription). The prosecutor went on quoting, "Moreover, this book bears the bookplate of Mark Samuels Lasner, the leading collector and authority on Max Beerbohm." I said I didn't know Mark Samuels Lasner personally but had heard of him. Boy, was it nice to hear that at least one of my signatures was legitimate.

Then suddenly the interview took on a more serious tone. The prosecutor wanted to know whether I had sold any other Osgood books or whether I intended to sell any of these books. The implication was that if I did so with a knowledge of their being forged, this would make me a conspirator in Osgood's (and this goddam Nevins') alleged crimes. I said "Absolutely not." My lawyer said, very forcefully, "My client is a private collector and has never sold a book in his life, except for books he traded for credit with Osgood against the purchase of signed copies of the books in question. He did in good faith buy inscribed books from Osgood, books that he had not the slightest idea were falsely inscribed." Reiner said that I was a victim and that in due course I would be joining the dealers in a civil suit for damages against Osgood, depending on the outcome of this criminal investigation. The FBI man then asked why I did not come forward when I first learned of Osgood being investigated, and I said that I didn't know the signatures were bad until I was informed by this office. I admitted I was hoping (maybe against hope) that my inscriptions were authentic. I said I realized now it would have been better had I contacted the authorities two or three weeks ago, but how was I to know my inscriptions were fake?

I thought I "performed" pretty well despite my nerves. After all, I was no goddam conspirator of any kind. I thought they were satisfied, and we actually shook hands and I left with that one Beerbohm book with the uncontested signature and the Lasner bookplate.

Afterwards, my lawyer spoke privately with the prosecutor, who said that he believed me, and that I was not under any suspicion – "at least at this point," the bastard added – but Reiner said this was just legalese and he (Reiner) need not have mentioned it to me. I'm clear. Reiner said that if the case went to trial and Osgood/Nevins were ordered to pay restitution, I would be among those being compensated.

Later, talking with Reiner, I thought of something I could have said – in regard to that one legitimate Beerbohm inscription Osgood sold me. I remembered this too late. (Irving Gross had once acquainted me with the phrase l'esprit de l'escalier – thinking of some bright answer after it is too late and you are out of the room and going down the staircase.) Well, here's my staircase story: it struck me that this Beerbohm book was the only inscribed copy I bought from Osgood that he already had in stock. The others were obtained after I told him the titles I was looking for. He simply took my want list and three or four weeks later, with help from this Nevins, came up with just what the doctor ordered. The really big mystery is why Osgood bothered to deal with my books, small potatoes compared to his usual big-time business. Maybe he just loved the fun of pulling off such crimes.

And, Christ, think about this: what if Osgood had given me back the very same copy – signed now – that I had traded in for credit? Would I have spotted it? I was just so happy to get those inscribed copies that it never dawned on me to check, because I had not the slightest suspicion of anything like that. He could have even disguised his doings by putting in a

228

few new negative points, like a tiny tear or two in a dust jacket where there was none before, or by adding a former owner's name to the front fly lead. That would have definitely put me off the scent. Could he actually have pulled off such a stunt?

Ain't it a life? But I feel the ordeal is over — and you were right that I should not have been overdoing the worrying all these weeks. Good old Harold Ross, another great worrier, wrote to his daughter from his deathbed that "All worry is about the wrong thing." So, many thanks for all your "Don't worry" emails, even though they didn't have much effect here. But you were not entirely correct because it turned out that the prosecutor <u>did</u> have suspicions about me as a co-conspirator. What is it they say? — even paranoid persons can have enemies.

Larry

CHAPTER TWENTY-FOUR

From: L.Dickerson@verizon.net
To: Charlie.Dover@duquest.co.uk
May 14, 2013

Dear Charlie

It's me again, and it has nothing to do with Osgood, thank God. No, quite the contrary.

Are you all sitting down? Of course you are. But prepare yourself for something. About a week ago, I ordered a first edition of Max Beerbohm's The Happy Hypocrite on eBay from some place in Kent, England – for $356. But $356 was a very good price for The Happy Hypocrite, something that early and that rare. Moreover, although almost all surviving copies are falling apart, this one is intact. As you know, it's really not a book, it's a booklet, a fairy tale. The blank page after the cover was stuck to the half-title page. But be patient as I am almost shaking trying to type this. Well, when I got the blank page and the half-title page unstuck, there was an inscription on the blank page facing the half-title page:

> For Oscar Wilde
> Yours Max
> May '97

Can you believe it? I know Oscar Wilde is a big deal, and anything connected to him gets huge prices. Am I right? He is the martyr and kind of the grandfather to the gay rights movement, and I am pleased to have something connected to him. Remember, Charlie, how you and I emailed about the Sotheby's sale of an Oscar Wilde book inscribed to Bobbie Ross that went for $363,000. My book is not from Wilde, of course, but still.

Larry

I'm forwarding this same message to Irving and Spencer. But I just had to share this Wilde business first with you because I knew how much you would appreciate it.

As for my "Total outlay to date" – the hell with it, though I can't help recording it here, namely $36,016 – or one grand past my $5,000 limit for this second year – after that extravagant first year of $30,000. On the other hand, if I get restitution, I'll be in much better shape.

*

From: Charlie.Dover@duquest.co.uk
To: L.Dickerson@verizon.net
15 May 2013

Dear Larry,

What wonderful news! I am almost tempted to use two exclamation marks. You deserve some wonderful news, given your recent problems with Osgood and with nine of your inscribed copies turning out to be forgeries. And even before that, you had other setbacks (I have a good memory for such things): those "early" Trollopes that proved worthless; that useless three-decker by an unknown; the ex-library copy; overpaying for Tess of the D'Urbervilles; some condition issues you were unaware of at first, etc. But especially of course all the worry and grief which that Osgood business put you through. So it was about time the book gods shone upon you with this singular stroke of good luck. Extravagant good luck, really. An early Beerbohm inscription to Oscar Wilde. This is "big time." It will be the jewel in the crown of your (renewed) collection. It would be a jewel in any private collection.

I'm very happy for you.

Charlie

* * *

From: smeans101@aol.com
To: L.Dickerson@verizon.net
May 15, 2013

Dear Larry

   Congratulations. The inscription is literally priceless, especially given its spectacular context.

Spencer

* * *

From: Irving.Gross@ns.edu
To: L.Dickerson@verizon.net
May 15, 2013

Dear Larry

Good for you! One can't do better than Oscar Wilde. I was about to say check the authenticity of the inscription. But that would only make you worry.

Irving

* * *

From: L.Dickerson@verizon.net
To: Charlie.Dover@duquest.co.uk
May 16, 2013

Dear Charlie,

232

I've managed to carefully open the page with the inscription and am sending you a scan now for your inspection. My pal Irving Gross was kind enough to suggest that I worry about authenticity, and God knows he's right, given all my troubles with Osgood. Give me your professional opinion as to authenticity. Also, and strictly off the record, can you give me some idea of its worth? Not that I mean to sell it.

Larry

I had to be damn careful not to break off the covers in getting this scan.

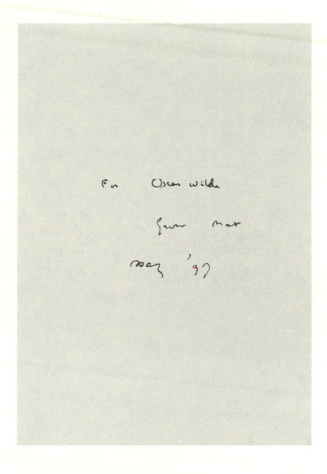

*

From: Charlie.Dover@duquest.co.uk
To: L.Dickerson@verizon.net
16 May, 2013

Dear Larry

The inscription you sent certainly looks genuine to me. But I'll check further for you, so you can be as close as possible to absolute assurance. I'll also work up some off the record estimate of its value at auction. This will take a few days.

Charlie

* * *

From: smeans101@aol.com
To: L.Dickerson@verizon.net
May 17, 2013

Dear Larry

   To follow up, are you are sure your copy is dated 1897 on the title page and reads "Copyright 1896" on the reverse of the title page? and that the Colophon (a kind of printer's statement at the back) reads "December m dccc xc vi"? Because if it were a later edition, the inscription would have to be fraudulent.

Spencer

*

From: L.Dickerson@verizon.net
To: smeans101@aol.com
May 17, 2013

Dear Spencer

    Sure I'm sure. At least I think I am. On the last page it says "December m dccc xc vi" — so actually it was printed in 1896, if I have my Roman numbers straight.

Larry

*

From: smeans101@aol.com
To: L.Dickerson@verizon.net
May 18, 2013

Dear Larry

    Then it's a genuine first all right. That helps authenticate the inscription, with its spectacular context.

Spencer

No news on the Osgood front?

*

From: L.Dickerson@verizon.net
To: smeans101@aol.com
May 18, 2013

Dear Spencer

   That's twice now that you mentioned its "spectacular" context. Can
you tell me just what you mean? All I know is Max Beerbohm and Wilde
were friends. Not the closest, but friends.

                              Larry

No, no news on Osgood. I am trying my best to put the whole business
out of my mind. But this new development tops everything, including him.

                              *

From: smeans101@aol.com
To: L.Dickerson@verizon.net
May 19, 2013

Dear Larry

   Granted your friend at Christie's is right on the authenticity of the
inscribed booklet, you have in your possession just about the most
remarkable inscription imaginable from Max Beerbohm because of the
very particular circumstances surrounding Max's sending the booklet to
Wilde.
   As for the latter, I open Halderin's Yale biography and type out for you
the context of that inscription of <u>The Happy Hypocrite</u>.
   Oscar Wilde was for some years the lover of young Lord Alfred
"Bosie" Douglas. Bosie's father, the Marquis of Queensberry (the rules of
boxing man) was infuriated at them and left a card at the Albemarle Club,
"For Oscar Wilde posing somdomite." (Note the misspelling: lords didn't
bother about spelling.) Wilde, foolishly, sued Queensberry for libel.
   The jury ruled for Queensberry. Revelations at the trial led to Wilde's

arrest for indecency and sodomy. Max, back from abroad, attended this second trial and wrote to Reggie Turner that Wilde, on the stand, said that "the love that dare not speak its name was such great affection of an older man for a younger man as there was between David and Jonathan, such as Plato made the very basis of his philosophy, and such as you find in the sonnets of Michelangelo and Shakespeare." Max says Wilde "carried the whole court away." This second trial ended in a hung jury. Another trial was scheduled, and between trials Max visited the police inspector who had arrested Wilde, hoping for "amelioration of some kind," and in the policeman's office he saw pinned up on the wall a copy of one of his cruel caricatures of Wilde. Seeing this made Max feel that he had "contributed to the dossier against Oscar." Here's a scan.

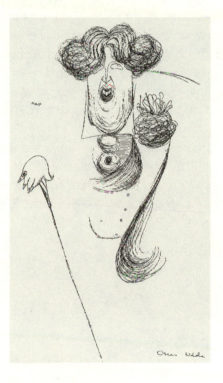

The third trial led to Wilde's conviction and a sentence of two years' hard labor. While Oscar was in jail Max published his first book The Works of Max Beerbohm, and a fairy tale called The Happy Hypocrite. In May 1897 Wilde was released from prison and left immediately for Dieppe in France where Bobbie Ross and Reggie Turner received him; Turner wrote to Max, telling him of preparations they had made: "In his room we have put a lot of flowers. All the books we have collected are on the mantel piece and your own two works are in the centre to catch his eye."

Shortly thereafter Wilde wrote to Turner, "I have just read Max's The Happy Hypocrite, beginning at the end, as one should always do. It is quite wonderful, and to one who was once known as the author of Dorian Gray full of no surprises of style or incident." Then Wilde wrote to Max:

> I cannot tell you what a real pleasure it was for me to find your delightful present waiting for me on my release from prison and to receive the charming and sweet messages you sent me. The Happy Hypocrite is a wonderful and beautiful story though I do not like the cynical directness of the name.... But in years to come, when you are a very young man, you will remember what I have said and recognize its truth, and in the final edition of your work leave the title unchanged. The implied and accepted recognition of Dorian Gray in the story cheers me. I had always been disappointed that my story had suggested no other work of art in others.

Wilde died in Paris in 1900 tended by Turner and Ross.

Well now, Larry, if you really have that copy of The Happy Hypocrite, and it appears that you do, you have a priceless artifact in your hands. It's perfectly wonderful. Congratulations. You deserve it. Especially after that awful Osgood business.

Spencer

From: L.Dickerson@verizon.net
To: smeans101@aol.com
May 19, 2013

Dear Spencer

Jesus Christ Almighty, I don't deserve it. But thank you for all the dope
on Wilde. I can't believe you wrote all that out for me. Well, I can believe
it because I have your email right in front of me. Thanks a million. To think
that I have that copy of The Happy Hypocrite! Maybe I'm a happy
hypocrite myself. In any case, I'm damned happy. The thing is priceless,
you say. Priceless? I'm inquiring of my lady friend at Christie's what that
might exactly mean, or what it might approximately mean.

Larry

* * *

From: L.Dickerson@verizon.net
To: Charlie.Dover@duquest.co.uk
May 19, 2013

Dear Charlie

I don't owe this eBay guy anything, do I?
I forward to you a long email from Spencer Means, laying out the
context of this copy of The Happy Hypocrite. Also I forward to you a
scan of the 1894 Oscar Wilde caricature that Spencer Means mentioned.

Larry

*

239

From: Charlie.Dover@duquest.co.uk
To: L.Dickerson@verizon.net
21 May 2013

Dear Larry

Absolutely, you do not owe the seller anything. If it's caveat emptor, it's also caveat vendor.

Your friend Spencer Means must be a very generous man to type all that out for you instead of just telling you to look it up.

The inscription and signature certainly look good to me and to one of my colleagues. Off the record and based unofficially on the scan you sent, I would suggest auction estimates of $15,000–$25,000. It could very well go higher if Wilde and or Beerbohm fanatics were bidding against each other.

Given your past worries on signatures in regard to those nine bad books Osgood sold you, I suggest you get in touch with Mark Samuels Lasner. He's the last word on Beerbohm and has helped us at Christie's to authenticate Beerbohm signatures and caricatures. You can locate him and his email at the University of Delaware Library. You mentioned having a Beerbohm book with Lasner's bookplate in it.

I'm very happy for you.

The other scan you forwarded to me of the caricature of Wilde the year before his trial is indeed "cruel," to say the least.

Charlie

*

From: L.Dickerson@verizon.net
To: Charlie.Dover@duquest.co.uk
May 21, 2013

Dear Charlie

Unbelievable – your estimates.

I certainly trust your judgment on authenticity, but since you yourself suggest I double check with this Mark Samuels Lasner, I will. I'll start with an old-fashioned phone call.

This latest development makes me feel better about spending money on rare books. As to my "absolute" budget limit – the hell with it. And so much for worrying about going beyond $25,000 and then $30,000 for the first year, and then $5,000 for this year, and bothering you with all those running totals. For one thing, that $35,000 is just about 9% of $400,000. This figure of 9% isn't at all a "round number." So why not say $40,000? That of course is a nice round ten percent. And I may start collecting a few drawings, something I've been thinking about for a long time now.

                                    Larry

Grand total to date: $36,367

                    *

From: L.Dickerson@verizon.net
To: Charlie.Dover@duquest.co.uk
May 23, 2013

Dear Charlie

Here's news! Reiner the lawyer just called and told me that Osgood has entered a guilty plea in federal court, with the prosecutor agreeing to recommend a lighter sentence when the case comes before a sentencing judge. I asked Reiner what kind of sentence he thought Osgood would get. Reiner could only conjecture, but he figures Osgood might get a few years in prison instead of many years. He just might get home confinement, but Reiner said that was unlikely.

And although the bad books he sold to these other dealers and individuals amount to a pretty penny (and other dealers have also now come forward), you really wonder, again, why in God's name Osgood would bother with relatively inexpensive books like those he sold to me.

Nevins's case is still pending.

As far as restitution goes, Reiner says the judge by law will order <u>full</u> restitution! When it rains it pours – this news on top of my Beerbohm/ Oscar Wilde inscription. I'll start collecting those books that had the faked inscriptions all over again. Besides, the fun is in the hunt, right? We don't know if "full" restitution will be for the 16K or the 11K (for only the actual dollars laid out, that is, not giving me back anything for the books I traded in.) And frankly, m'dear, at this point I don't give a damn.

Larry

*

From: Charlie.Dover@duquest.co.uk
To: L.Dickerson@verizon.net
24 May 2013

Dear Larry

Congratulations. Good news indeed. Now for the Mark Samuels Lasner verdict. I'm pretty convinced I know what it will be.

Charlie

* * *

From: Msl@udel.edu
To: L.Dickerson@verizon.net
May 25, 2013

Dear Larry Dickerson

Thanks for your telephone call. Your inscribed <u>Happy Hypocrite</u> sounds
like something I myself would have coveted beyond the dreams of lust or
avarice. But it is good that another collector, a new one, has such a
precious item. I presume my verdict will concur with Christie's, namely,
that the inscription is authentic. But I must see it first.

I again commiserate with you about Osgood. I myself – who did most of
my collecting years ago – have never had any dealings with Osgood.

Send me the scan. And your phone number.

Yours sincerely
Mark

Mark Samuels Lasner
Senior Research Fellow
University of Delaware Library
Newark DE 19711

From: L.Dickerson@verizon.net
To: Msl@udel.edu
May 25, 2013

Dear Mark

  Thanks for agreeing to look at this. Here's the scan, and my telephone
number, 212 473 1927.
  I'll be waiting by the phone.

                                                    Yours
                                                    Larry

                      *   *   *

From: L.Dickerson@verizon.net
To: Charlie.Dover@duquest.co.uk
May 25, 2013

Dear Charlie

  Mark Samuels Lasner called me back. He says, "Larry, I'm looking at the
scan you sent, from your copy of The Happy Hypocrite." Then he paused.
Then he continued, "I've looked at it very carefully and have compared the
words within the inscription with manuscripts I have." Another pause. I felt
like a patient waiting for a doctor to tell you the results of some goddam
x-ray, whether your lungs are healthy or filled with cancer or something. I
went on holding my breath, and also thinking what the hell am I going to
say if he thinks it's a forgery. But he didn't. He said that this was the kind
of thing he would have killed for. (He didn't sound like a killer.) I let my
breath out and thanked him profusely. He said no call for thanks, really, he
was simply giving his opinion. Seeing that he is the world's authority on
Max's handwriting, I could only say, well, thanks again anyway. He sounds
like a very nice guy. I like to think I would have liked him even if he had
questioned the authenticity of the inscription – but I doubt it.

Then he launched into a discussion of how he just <u>loves</u> inscribed copies. He says an inscription makes a copy unique. He is much more interested in rarity, or "uniqueness," than in the value of a famous book. He tells me there are many copies of the Chelmscott <u>Chaucer</u> around – he said he could make three phone calls and have three copies on his desk tomorrow. Similarly, even for early Shakespeare First Folios (not true firsts), there are enough around so that even at "stratospheric" prices he does not consider these as truly "rare" books – just <u>expensive</u> ones. At this point I was hoping to get off the phone and send you the news.

I'm so anxious for you to have this news, first – the first among all my advisers. And you of course suggested contacting Mark Samuels Lasner. I will tell all my other book pals next.

I'm going to get in touch with the owner of that Rossetti caricature.

And tell me when those Beerbohm drawings (or any Thurber) are coming up for auction at Christie's London. Melanie and I will be coming to London. I've put it off long enough.

XOXO
Larry

I'm also splurging on dinner tonight, taking Melanie to that fancy restaurant down here on East 12th Street, the Gotham Bar and Grill. Very expensive. What the hell. I feel like a new man. Whatever exactly that means.

A NOTE ON THE TYPE

Bibliophilia has been set in Gill Sans Nova, a reissue of a 1928 design commissioned from the lettering artist and sculptor Eric Gill by Stanley Morison for Monotype. Long a favorite of designers and readers, Gill Sans possesses a readability and warmth often missing in geometric sans-serifs like Futura and grotesques like Helvetica. While Gill's oversight and influence were essential in the earliest versions of the types intended for machine composition, later versions were redrawn after Gill's death, and iterations intended for photo-composition and digital typesetting strayed (sometimes rather far) from the originals. In 2014, George Ryan — senior type designer at Monotype — took on the task of updating the existing patchwork of types, redrawing characters, introducing new weights, and expanding the glyph sets. The result is a fresh take on a classic humanist sans-serif type that ranks high among the great type designs of the twentieth century.

DESIGN & COMPOSITION BY CARL W. SCARBROUGH